John & Dear Russell Lyndsey
& Lyndsey
Dassley

OPENING SALVO

It was a mistake for Mary Lawrence to go with Lord Rule into the moonlit garden. And a graver one to think her biting wit could keep him under control.

"I am done playing games with you, Miss Lawrence," he declared. "You tell me I am no gentleman, yet I have only your word for it that you are a lady."

"Wh-What are you going to do?" she asked.

"What do you think I'm going to do?" Lord Rule returned in a soft growl.

"No!" Mary protested swiftly, but not nearly quickly enough to keep her denial from being smothered by Lord Rule's punishing mouth. Nor did her hands move rapidly enough to prevent his arms from capturing her slim body in his rock-hard embrace.

Decidedly Mary was being bested in this first skirmish with the ruthless Lord Rule—and unless she came up with a new defense, she would soon lose all. . . .

D0288164

SIGNET REGENCY ROMANCE
COMING IN JULY 1993

Gayle Buck
Miss Dower's Paragon

Dorothy Mack
The Lost Heir

Dawn Lindsey
The Reluctant Heroine

Laura Matthews
In My Lady's Chamber

AT YOUR LOCAL BOOKSTORE
OR ORDER DIRECTLY
FROM THE PUBLISHER
WITH VISA OR MASTERCARD
1-800-253-6476

The Ruthless Lord Rule

Michelle Kasey

A SIGNET BOOK

To Page—
the Consummate Miss Cuddy—
who let me be me; with deep gratitude and affection

SIGNET
Published by the Penguin Group
Penguin Books USA Inc., 375 Hudson Street,
New York, New York 10014, U.S.A.
Penguin Books Ltd, 27 Wrights Lane,
London W8 5TZ, England
Penguin Books Australia Ltd, Ringwood,
Victoria, Australia
Penguin Books Canada Ltd, 10 Alcorn Avenue,
Toronto, Ontario, Canada M4V 3B2
Penguin Books (N.Z.) Ltd, 182–190 Wairau Road,
Auckland 10, New Zealand

Penguin Books Ltd, Registered Offices:
Harmondsworth, Middlesex, England

Published by Signet, an imprint of New American Library,
a division of Penguin Books USA Inc.

First Printing, October, 1987
11 10 9 8 7 6 5 4 3

Copyright © Kathryn Seidick 1987
All rights reserved

Ⓢ REGISTERED TRADEMARK—MARCA REGISTRADA

Printed in the United States of America

BOOKS ARE AVAILABLE AT QUANTITY DISCOUNTS WHEN USED TO PROMOTE PRODUCTS OR
SERVICES. FOR INFORMATION PLEASE WRITE TO PREMIUM MARKETING DIVISION, PENGUIN
BOOKS USA INC., 375 HUDSON STREET, NEW YORK, NEW YORK 10014.

If you purchased this book without a cover you should be aware that this book is stolen
property. It was reported as "unsold and destroyed" to the publisher and neither the
author nor the publisher has received any payment for this "stripped book."

March 1814

Peace!

All England is rejoicing. Napoleon, that scourge of the Continent, has at last been put in his cage. Paris has capitulated, with the trusted Marmont leading his unsuspecting men straight into the Austrian camp in surrender. Now an emperor in name only, with but a scant four-hundred-man army and living on the charity of the country he had led in triumph for nearly twenty years, Bonaparte barely escaped France with his life and is living in genteel poverty on the unpretentious island of Elba.

His Royal Highness, the Prince Regent, is delirious with joy; so overcome that he'd had to be bled of twenty-seven ounces of blood. Indeed, for nearly a month, he languished in his bed, hovering between life and death.

The rush to cross the Channel is already in full force, with even the Duke of Wellington, now British ambassador to France, characteristically ignoring the angry glances cast his way as he saunters down the streets of Paris, dines on good, plain English fare at the Café des Anglais, and accepts the grateful thanks of the repatriated French nobility.

London is in a whirl, eagerly anticipating the arrival of Czar Alexander of Russia, King Frederick William of Prussia, and, wonder of wonders, the much loved Field Marshal von Blücher. Indeed, the Grand Duchess Catherine of Oldenburg, the czar's "platter-faced" sister, has already disembarked and is royally ensconced in Pulteney's Hotel, busily setting up the Regent's back with her Whig antics.

That this endears her to the residents of London is no surprise, for the Regent has been out of favor with his subjects for some time. The younger generation has no memory of the glorious Florizel that was once the Prince of Wales and cannot think of him as the genial Big Ben. They see him instead as Swellfoot, an obese, grotesque, thoroughly evil man. They glory in the little ditty penned by Charles Lamb:

> By his bulk and by his size,
> By his oily qualities,
> This (or else my eyesight fails)
> This should be the Prince of *Whales*.

Not that Louix XVIII, who had been cheered through the streets as he headed toward the Channel Ports and a return to his homeland, fared much better once he reached Paris. The King, whom Lord Byron has irreverently dubbed Louis the Gouty, seems to have spent his entire exile in thrall with his host country's cooking, and is so thoroughly corpulent that the Regent, after investing the King with the Order of the Garter, and buckling the Garter around a leg even thicker than his own, remarked, "When I clasped his knee it was exactly as if I were fastening a sash around a young man's waist."

One German account of the King's appearance commented on both the advanced age and accumulated fat of Napoleon's replacement. Telling of the King's entrance into the room, the report centered on the fact that Louis, clad in soft black satin boots and supported on either side, was so disablingly obese that he "would stumble over a straw."

While Europe laughs at reports of Napoleon's frugal inventories of mattresses and his drawing up of lists of his personal clothing ("my underlinen is in a lamentable state"), and ridicules his official-sounding Council of State that he has set up to investigate improvements in the iron mines and salt pits of Elba while considering the possibility of importing silkworms, the banished Emperor is reading of the high jinks being perpetrated by his vanquishers.

"They are mad!" he said of the governments that had a hand in putting Louis on the throne. "The Bourbons in France; they would not be able to hold their position for a year! Nine-tenths of the nation cannot endure them; my soldiers will never serve under them."

But none of the leaders of the world, their minds filled with plans for pomp and ceremony and grand celebrations, hear the words of Napoleon Bonaparte, or, if they do hear them, heed them.

Only a few shake their heads at the merrymaking and wonder—wonder if this glorious peace is really to be believed. Sir Henry Ruffton, one of the War Office's most intelligent members, wonders.

Then word reaches Sir Henry of one of Bonaparte's final statements before leaving France. "Between ourselves," Napoleon has told a trusted aide who had feared his Emperor would commit suicide, "a living drummer is better than a dead emperor."

So, while London rings with cheers and hangs bunting from the façades, Sir Henry pens two messages. One missive goes to Sussex by private courier. The other is sent by packet to Calais, to his most trusted operative. Both messages are the same: "Come to me, now."

CHAPTER ONE

May 1814

"Honestly, Mary, that new coachman of Sir Henry's drives as if he's riding to hounds." Gratefully subsiding into a chair in the rather spartanly furnished drawing room, Rachel Gladwin removed her straw bonnet and proceeded to use it as a fan to cool her flushed cheeks. "While I applaud your guardian's hiring of returned soldiers, I do believe he should temper his generosity with a bit of common sense. I doubt if even Wellington would have survived if all of our troop charges into battle were accomplished with the same reckless fervor our driver just demonstrated on Bond Street."

Pushing at the dark coppery curls that had been slightly crushed by her fetching, if a bit imprudent, choice of headgear, Mary Lawrence smiled into the mirror that reflected Rachel's frowning face. "Coming it a bit too brown, aren't you, Aunt?" she asked, using the courtesy title that lady had insisted upon, "considering it was you who applauded so enthusiastically when that same driver sent that ridiculous dandy scurrying up the lamppost in fear of his life?"

Rachel's features relaxed into a small smile. "I will admit to being a bit amused by the spectacle," she owned cheerfully enough, "but I would be shirking my duty as your resident bear-leader if I did not stress once again that putting one's fingers in one's mouth and whistling encouragement to servants is just *not done*. Wherever did you acquire such a disgusting talent, Mary?"

"In Sussex," Mary Lawrence replied, leaving the mirror to take up residence in the chair across from Rachel's. "You'd be surprised at the accomplishments I have mastered through the kind offices of my last keepers, may they live long and prosper. And you are not bear-leading me, no one could. You are my friend and companion while I'm forced to live in London."

Rachel shook her head. "Still singing the same sad song, Mary? I thought Sir Henry had succeeded in convincing you that this is the best, the safest, place for you at the moment."

"Bah! All the world is in Paris. The papers are full of *on-dits* about the English lords and ladies who are scampering about France, aping the latest fashions and gambling away their fortunes at the Palais-Royal—among other things," she ended, winking broadly. "I fail to see why Sir Henry refuses to let me cross the Channel. It's so dreadfully flat here; I was better entertained in Sussex."

Looking at the very young, very beautiful girl dressed in the height of fashion, a girl who in her few short weeks in the metropolis had already been dubbed the latest Incomparable, Rachel suppressed a chuckle and tried for a commiserating tone. "La, you poor, oppressed creature. Forced to spend your time dragging yourself from ballroom to theater party, your unwilling body pressed into wearing an endless array of flattering silks and satins, while saddled with the unpalatable chore of breaking every young male heart in London. I daresay I admire you for not dissolving on your bed in a flood of tears, so onerous is your trial."

Mary screwed up her patrician nose and stuck out her tongue. "Wretch! You know I'm loving every delicious minute of it. It's just that I should love it even more if I were doing it in Paris. Besides—surely *he* wouldn't be so odious as to follow me there to make my life miserable."

"Ah, we're back to that, are we?" Rachel chuckled, shaking her head. "My nephew seems to have gotten under your skin."

"Like an annoying splinter," Mary admitted irritably. "How that insufferable man dogs my every step! If you're afraid of the way our coachman drives, *I* am fearful that your odious nephew is doing to drive *me*—into strong hysterics. Are you quite sure he wasn't a soldier, perhaps suffering from some head injury that makes him behave so toward me?"

"Tristan was never a soldier, Mary," Rachel replied, crossing her fingers in her lap. "There have been rumors about his actions during the war, but I discount them. No, my nephew is just being his usual annoying self."

Mary looked closely at her companion. "You sound as if you don't like him. Not that I blame you, of course, for he does not wear easily."

Rachel smiled sadly. "Not like him? Why, Mary, I couldn't love him more. Tris is loyal, trustworthy, unflinchingly honest, and the staunchest friend a person could ever have."

"I once had a terrier with the same attributes." Mary sniffed derisively. "Only he was better trained. All your nephew seems to have mastered is the ability to heel! Besides, if Lord Rule is such a paragon of virtue, why do you always give such a deep sigh when you see him? Seems rather unloving to me."

Now the older woman laughed aloud. "Because he's such a royal pain in the rump, Mary dearest, why else?"

Mary decided to change the subject, as their discussion of the Right Honorable Baron Rule was fast beginning to give her the headache. She rose and walked over to take the card rack down from the mantel, meaning to sort out the cards of invitation for the one she needed for that evening. "We're expected at Lady Salerton's for her daughter's come-out. Shall I wear my yellow tiffany?"

"Not unless you want Elsie Salerton to throw her not unimpressive bulk against the door to bar you from entering. Really, Mary, can you not let the poor girl have her evening without spoiling it by ensnaring every young buck her mother is bound to have cajoled, blackmailed, or bludgeoned into appearing?"

Mary smiled, showing up the very fetching dimple in her left cheek, then batted her large, wide green eyes innocently. "Why, Aunt, whatever do you mean? I merely enjoy dancing and chatting with people my own age. Anyone would think you believe me to be a heartless flirt." Her smile fading, she added, "Besides, once your dear nephew, Lord Rule, comes on the scene—which I am sure he will do as he seems to have an uncanny knack for knowing exactly which entertainment I have chosen for the evening—all my intrepid dancing partners will depart posthaste for the hinterlands, their tails between their legs."

"Maybe he's developed a *tendre* for you, dear," Rachel offered without much hope of being taken seriously.

"Not surprising. Who *hasn't* fallen head over ears for my beautiful ward?"

"Uncle Henry!" Mary cried, running across the room to give her guardian an enthusiastic hug. "Aunt Rachel has told me you have gotten us vouchers for Almack's. However did you manage it?"

The gray-haired, rosy-cheeked cherub who stood smiling inanely while his adored ward embraced him was Sir Henry Ruffton, a wealthy bachelor on the shady side of forty with a reputation as a truly guileless, completely lovable soul. That he had the total admiration of his ward was obvious, and he felt the years fall away from him as he basked in her affection. "Silly puss, who could afford to ignore such a diamond of the first water as you? Not Lady Jersey, that much is certain. Besides, I do have a smattering of friends who were not adverse to pulling a few strings in the right places."

Rachel watched the scene unfolding in front of her, a sad smile on her face. Mary could have been his daughter, could have been *their* daughter, if only . . . "Henry, I do believe you're blushing!" she teased, rising to ring for refreshments.

Seating himself in his favorite chair, allowing Mary to curl up on the floor at his feet, her head pressed against his knees, Sir Henry acknowledged Rachel's words unself-consciously. "I admit it, Rachel, my dear friend. I have not been so diverted in years. Having Mary join me in the city was truly an inspiration. And finding you after all this time to act as companion and chaperon, why there are times I believe myself to be the happiest of men."

"Don't forget that the war is over, Uncle," Mary pointed out. "That's another reason for you to be happy."

"Napoleon is within spitting distance of Europe, child," he answered, suddenly looking something less than cherubic. "I cannot help but agree with Talleyrand, who fought to have Bonaparte exiled in Corfu, or even St. Helena, where he could be more closely guarded."

"Piffle," Mary argued. "Fouché, I've heard, suggeted Boney flee to America and start over. I wonder how the Americans would have taken to that notion. Besides, Talleyrand is no good authority. I have read that Napoleon once called him 'filth in silk stockings.' "

"Talleyrand is an amoral thief, Mary, but he hasn't survived in France this long without being a fairly good judge of men. If he says Bonaparte still presents a danger, I tend to believe him."

"But—"

"Enough, child. You make my head buzz with all your silly prattle. I have given you my reasons and you have agreed to abide by my decision. Once some time has passed, and the governments conclude their deliberations, perhaps then I shall set you off to France with my blessing. I may even accompany you. But for now—"

"But for now I am safer in London," Mary ended fatalistically. "But all this pretense, I vow I cannot like it. Even my name—"

"*Perkins!*" Rachel interrupted rather loudly, startling the butler into nearly oversetting the tray of tea and cakes. "How famished I am. If you would set the tray on this table I'm sure we shall be able to serve ourselves quite well unaided. Thank you, Perkins."

Mary watched the butler's departing back, a rueful smile on her lips. "I almost gave it away just then, didn't I, Aunt? Thank you for your timely intervention." Then, momentarily feeling mulish, she added, "Though I still think this whole deception is silly."

Rachel and Sir Henry exchanged knowing looks over Mary's head and pretended not to hear her last statement. Biting into a warm scone, Sir Henry questioned, "Which one of Mary's suitors were you discussing when I entered the room? It's getting to the point where I have to keep a list with me at all times so that I may check them off when I am forced to turn down their requests for her hand."

Mary thrust her full lower lip forward into a pout. "Lord Tristan Rule, Uncle Henry, and he is not a suitor. He's a nuisance!"

"Tristan?" Sir Henry repeated, puzzled. "I've never known him to be in the petticoat line. My congratulations, my dear, he's a fine young man."

Mary leaped to her feet and glared at her beloved guardian. "If you have any affection for that fine young man, you will steer him swiftly away from my direction before I skewer him with my parasol! I cannot stand the creature!"

And with that, Mary quit the room, stopping only to snatch up a few fragrant scones, leaving Rachel to explain Lord Rule's recent behavior to Sir Henry.

Tristan Rule reached down a hand to assist his opponent to his feet. "Sorry, George. It seems my tiresome temper has gotten the better of me again."

"On the contrary," Lord Byron replied, gingerly rubbing his aching jaw, "it was my fault entirely. I should have known better than to cast aspersions on our esteemed War Office while sparring with Ruthless Rule. Besides, I thought I had a better chin than I seem to possess. Just remember, Tris, the pen is mightier than the sword. I'll simply have to scribble a canto or two someday about our esteemed military gentlemen." Stepping out between the ropes held apart by his friend, Byron called out ruefully, "Tom, my good man, you'd better look to your laurels now that Ruthless Rule is stepping into the ring. I do believe he would make even you a fair competitor. Now toss me that towel and help me totter over to find a glass of wine, if you please."

Dexter Rutherford, who had been holding a towel at the ready for his idol, Lord Tristan Rule, dashed to the side of the ring, a look of slavish adoration on his young face. "What a leveler you served him, Tris!" he exclaimed, rubbing his hero's bare shoulders with more enthusiasm than expertise. "The great man himself, dropped by a single blow. What science, what speed, what—"

"What loss of control," Tristan ended crossly, effectively wiping the grin from Dexter's face. "We were only sparring, you bloodthirsty infant. George wasn't expecting that bit of home-brewed I served up to him. Thank goodness he's a gentleman." Taking the towel from his shoulders, Rule rubbed it briskly across his face and neck. "It's this deuced inaction. I feel like a coiled wire ready to spring. I can see that this peace everyone is so delirious about is going to take a bit of getting used to."

Tom Cribb, the retired "Champion Boxer of all England," approached the pair, a nearly full glass of wine held in front of him. "With Lord Byron's compliments, my lord. And may I say it was an honor to watch you in there. If you ever have a mind to go a few rounds, I wouldn't say no to you. Your right hand reminds me a bit of Ikey Pigg's, and I considered him a very worthy opponent in his day."

"Ikey Pigg!" Dexter cried scoffingly. "Molyneaux, more like, and it took you thirty rounds or more to best him too. Ikey Pigg?" Dexter shook his head. "Damned insult if you ask me."

"Nobody did, sprig," came a voice from behind the young man. "I'd say my good-byes now, if I were you, before Tom here takes it into his head to squash you like a bug."

Dexter whirled to greet his cousin. "Julian! Did you see him? It was nothing next to marvelous, I tell you. One moment Lord Byron was standing there, his fives at the ready, and the next he was rump down on the mat, with Lord Rule standing above him, breathing fire."

"Sorry we missed it," Julian Rutherford, Earl of Thorpe, mourned falsely as he joined the group. "Yet somehow I feel that we shall all be able to relive the moment *ad nauseam* over dinner this evening if Dex here has anything to say in the matter." Julian turned to address Lord Rule as Tom Cribb drifted away to talk to some of his other patrons. "You haven't forgotten Lucy's invitation, have you? I'll have the devil to pay if I tell her I've seen you here without reminding you that your presence is required at table."

"Not to mention what Jennie will do to me," Kit Wilde, Earl of Bourne, put in as he too joined the small group, barely concealing a smile as he thought of his wife. "Your cousins are both rare handfuls in their separate ways, Tris, as you must know."

"Will your aunt Rachel and her charge also be present?" Tris asked, slipping his arms into the shirt Dexter was holding up for him.

"Mary Lawrence?" Julian asked rhetorically, winking slyly at Kit, who was hiding a grin behind his hand. "So it's true, what Lucy and Jennie say? I warn you, they've as much as made a match of it between you."

Tris looked blank, as indeed he was at a loss to understand what Lord Thorpe was talking about. "Make a match of it? With Mary Lawrence? What in blazes put a fool notion like that into their maggoty heads?"

"Not just them, Tris," Dexter supplied with all the innocence his ignorance of the world provided him. "Saw it in the betting book at Boodle's. At least three wagers on when the announcement will make the *Morning Chronicle*."

Tris snorted. "The *Morning Chronicle*—as if

anyone would believe anything James Perry has to say in that paper of his. Why, I read one of his 'stories' just the other day that told of Prinny being applauded as he passed through the streets. As if being hissed at and having your coach pelted with cabbages can be called acclamation. Give me the *Times*, thank you. At least John Walter could be trusted to keep the war news straight." Then, belatedly getting down off his high ropes, he gave a bit of thought to just what Dexter had said. "Betting on me at Boodle's, are they? Who, damn it? Give me names, boy, and I'll call the bastards out, damned if I won't!"

"That's it, Tris, keep a cool head, just like you're known to do," Lord Bourne jibed, placing an arm around the other man's shoulders. "Besides, you have no one to blame but yourself, the way you act whenever the chit enters a room. Can't remember being so dashed silly about Jennie, even when she was leading me around like a puppy longing for a pat on the head."

Rule retied his cravat with more intensity than flair, his dark eyes flashing in a way that made Dexter decidedly nervous. "I only stand up with the girl for a single dance in an evening. I don't see where that should serve to set the world to hearing wedding bells."

Now it was time for Kit to wink at Julian. "I see your point, Tris. How like society to jump headlong to the wrong conclusion. Just because you show up everywhere Miss Lawrence happens to be as regularly as the sun rises every morning and claim her for a dance before retiring to a pillar and staring a hole in her back for the remainder of the evening. Imagine Lucy and Jennie, for instance, being so rash as to put any credence in the silly coincidence that you always quit the room just as soon as Miss Lawrence retires, or the fact that more than one young buck has reportedly withdrawn from the lists of those seeking the lady's favors due to the belief that you would call them out if they so much as looked in her direction." Lord Bourne shook his head sadly. "How sorely your motives are misinterpreted. What, precisely, then *are* your motives, Tris, if you aren't smitten?"

Rule answered with some questions of his own. "Who exactly *is* Mary Lawrence? Where does she come from? Who are her parents? What is she doing in London? Why is she living with Sir Henry Ruffton? My Aunt Rachel may be the girl's chaperon but she's as close as an oyster whenever I try to get a few answers out of her. I know about her botched engagement with Sir Henry all those years ago, but could loyalty to an old beau cloud her judgment to the point where she'd allow herself to be involved in . . . never mind, George is getting ready to leave. I really must offer my apologies to him one more time. Excuse me, gentlemen. I'll see you later this evening."

Before either Julian or Kit could gainsay him, Tris was off, his long strides taking him swiftly across the room, the ever-present Dexter scampering to keep up with him.

"What the devil was all that in aid of?" Julian asked his cousin-in-law, who was looking no more enlightened than he. "Rachel told me he was a strange one, alluding to some secret association with the war effort, but I do believe the years of pressure have served to unhinge his mind. Did you ever hear such ridiculousness? Anyone would think he believes Sir Henry to be harboring a lady of ill repute, or a spy, or something. No, can't be a spy. After all, the war's over, isn't it?"

Kit was still watching Lord Rule, taking in his naturally belligerent stance and remembering how well the fellow had looked stripped to the waist. No soft London dandy was Tristan Rule. He had the look of a fighting man, even a Peninsula man, unless Kit missed his guess. Yet, for all the rumors about the man, no one could actually say Rule had ever been within a hundred miles of a battle. Strange, moody fellow. But a man of strong convictions for all that. And now he has a bee in his bonnet about Mary Lawrence. Kit turned to look at Julian, a thoughtful twist on his lips. "The war over, you say, Julian? For some of us, maybe. But not for *him*, it would appear." He took one last look at the man they called Ruthless Rule as the tall, black-clad figure strode toward the door. "I tell you, Julian, I'd give my matched bays for a glimpse inside Tristan Rule's head."

CHAPTER TWO

Lucy Gladwin Rutherford, Countess of Thorpe, had great hopes for this dinner party, hopes she was foolish enough to share with her beloved husband, Julian, who quickly tried to dash them.

Stopping in the midst of tying his cravat, Lord Thorpe looked in his wife's direction as she stood fiddling with the contents of his dressing table. "Miss Lawrence and your cousin Tris?" He would have shaken his head if the knot he was tying was not just then at a very critical stage. "You're fair and far out this time, my love. Kit and I broached the subject this afternoon at Cribb's Parlor with the man in question, and I'd say Tris's interest is anything but loverlike."

A twinkle entered Lucy's eyes. "Ah, then you noticed his partiality for her too. My cousin is *definitely* interested in Miss Lawrence. You just misread the signs. Tris is nearly always stupid when it comes to women—he probably said something totally negative, if I know him."

Giving his handiwork a last, satisfied look in the mirror, Julian turned to plant a kiss on his wife's forehead—while deftly removing his favorite pearl studs from her investigating hands. "I wouldn't say the man was stupid. Actually, thinking back on the conversation, I believe Tris is more than casually interested in the girl. But, no, it is most assuredly not with an eye to setting up his nursery."

Lucy interpreted her husband's words in exactly the wrong way. Her small face taking on a look of horror, she gasped, "Surely you don't think he intends to set her up as his light-o'-love? I won't believe it!"

"Such a fertile mind you have, Lucy. I fear I must begin rationing your consumption of Minerva Press novels," Julian threatened kindly, and then his features sobered. "To be serious for a moment, love, I do believe your cousin has taken some wild idea into his head about your Mary Lawrence, something to do with her ancestry. Is Tris by chance a bigoted sort?"

"Never!" Lucy protested, flopping into a nearby chair with total disregard for the gown it had taken her maid two hours to press. "I can't understand any of this, Julian. Surely you must be mistaken."

"Kit too?" he nudged, selecting a plain gold signet ring for his finger. "But don't go into a decline, dearest. Surely you and Jennie can find another young couple to work your matchmaking wiles on before the Season is over. What about Dexter?"

"That nodcock?" Lucy exclaimed, momentarily diverted. "He may be your cousin, but he's still the silliest thing on two legs. The way he has attached himself to Tris, why a person could wonder just how much of his feeling is hero worship and how much is—"

"Lucy! You fill me with dismay! You're not supposed to know about such things, much less talk about them."

She smiled up at him impishly. "Not even with my beloved husband, Julian? Don't be so stuffy."

Julian reached down and pulled his wife to her

feet and up against his chest. "I am never stuffy, madam, and I have had that reassurance from your own lips." He looked down into her upturned face and gave a bemused smile, glad he had not yet called his valet to help him into his formfitting evening coat. "Ah, yes, my dearest, those lovely, enticing lips."

Lucy was forced to don another gown, as her maid, once she caught sight of her mistress some half hour later, had dissolved into tears and retired to her cot, in no condition to wield a hot iron.

They were all ensconced around the gleaming mahogany table; the Earl of Bourne and his Jennie, Rachel Gladwin alongside young Dexter Rutherford—there to make up the numbers when Sir Henry pleaded another commitment—Lord and Lady Thorpe at the head and foot of the table, and Tristan Rule and Mary Lawrence smack beside each other on one side, just as Lucy had cunningly engineered the thing earlier.

Jennie was still wearing a benevolent smile, as she hadn't as yet had either the benefit of her husband's opinion on her matchmaking scheme or been able to speak alone with Lucy, who was not looking quite so chipper. Indeed, Lucy was looking almost solemn, and had been ever since Miss Lawrence, beautifully attired in pale green silk, had greeted the sight of Tristan Rule with an unenthusiastic "Oh, *you're* here."

For her part, Rachel, who had recently taken to plotting her first attempt at a novel of her own, had decided to view the barely veiled hostility her charge directed at her nephew as ink for her scribbling pen. How interesting it would be, she thought as she helped herself to a portion of stewed carp, to have a heroine who insists on ignoring her attraction for the hero. Perhaps, she mused idly, I shall have my heroine outrage her mercenary guardian by refusing to stand up with the hero at her come-out ball. Would Maria Edgeworth approve? Was it too farfetched? Rachel shrugged her shoulders and took another bite of carp.

If Mary had been privy to her companion's thoughts, she might have added her bit to the story, a little plot twist that had the heroine surreptitiously slipping a bit of poison into the hero's fricassee of tripe and then running off to the Continent to become the reigning toast of Paris. But then Mary's mind was at the moment too overcrowded with thoughts of the man sitting so intrudingly close to her right side to have much heart for solving anyone's problems but her own.

Look at him, she instructed herself as she ignored her filled plate. He even cuts his meat with a cool, meticulous care that makes my flesh crawl. And those hands—those hard, tanned hands with their long, straight fingers. Everything about him screams leashed power. *Ruthless.* How apt. Energy seems to flow from him like a never-ending stream. Rachel may think that he's interested in me. My suitors may think he's trying to cut them out for my hand. But I know better. I can feel the animosity that charges the air whenever he looks at me. Why does he dislike me so? Why is he making it his business to unnerve me with his unwanted, discomforting presence? And why, dear God, *why* must he be so maddeningly intriguing, so damnably handsome?

While Mary sat staring at her plate, precisely as if the fish that lay there had just winked in her direction, Tristan Rule was building himself into a temper—not a new experience, granted, but he could not in his memory recall another instance when a female of the species had been able to crawl so deeply under his skin. Maybe it was that bloody black velvet ribbon she had tied tightly around her neck, just like the ladies of a generation ago had worn red ribbons in sympathy with the French nobility that had lost their heads on Madame Guillotine.

Fashion, his saner self told him. Nothing of the kind, his suspicious self contradicted. That ribbon is just one more nail in her coffin, one more revealing slip that another, less discerning man, might overlook. She was *mocking* those dead Frenchmen, no more, no less. But it would take more than a bit of ribbon and an inconclusive inquiry into Miss Lawrence's background to convince Sir Henry that he had been made the victim of a Bonapartist sympathizer. It was time he made a move, time he took a more positive step than merely to observe her as she pulled the wool over society's eyes with her portrayal of a young miss in her first Season. He was determined to unmask her for what she was. Why in the fiend's name, he snarled inwardly, did she have to be so beautiful?

"I had not known that you would be here this evening, sir."

Tristan's fork halted halfway to his mouth as Mary's softly spoken words startled him. As she had made such a point of ignoring him while they waited for dinner to be announced, he had resigned himself to having his ear bent all through the meal by Dexter, who sat across from him but wasn't about to let any silly dictate of good manners keep him from talking nineteen to the dozen across the table if he so chose. "You didn't?" was all he responded, eyeing her smiling face closely as he sought to understand her seeming friendliness.

"No," she answered, her voice still quite low. "I saw you striding through the drizzle the other day in the park and had figured you to have developed lung fever at the very least by now."

Tristan decided to take her words literally. "What would make you think a bit of spring drizzle could lay me up by the heels?"

Mary shrugged delicately, almost Gallically, in Tristan's biased opinion. "Oh, I don't know. I guess that it's just that you are of an age that I would have expected you to have served in the war if you weren't afflicted with a weak chest or some other such hidden *weakness*. Lord Bourne served on the Peninsula, you know, and Lord Thorpe was very involved with the war effort in Parliament. But you—why, if rumors are to be believed, you spent the last several years traipsing about the Continent like some sort of sightseer. In places far removed from the fighting, that is."

Tristan laid his fork carefully on the edge of his plate. Turning his head slowly in her direction once more, he smiled dangerously, his straight white teeth clenched. "If you were a man, I would call you out for that, you know," he said in his low, husky voice, a voice that went well with his chiseled features, dark eyes, and darker hair.

Another woman would have fainted. Lord, any sane woman wouldn't have taunted him so in the first place! But Mary Lawrence was made of sterner, if somewhat more foolhardy, stuff. She kept her chin high and didn't so much as blink. "Name your seconds, sir," she dared recklessly, ignoring her rapidly beating heart. "Although you neatly circumvented serving in the war, I have no doubt you've stomach enough to shoot a woman."

Now Tristan's smile was downright evil. "Too messy by half, madam. I prefer to impale my opponents on my sword. Now, madam, if you're still game . . . ?"

There was no pretending she didn't catch the double entendre hidden in his words, and no way she could slap his face at Lucy's table without creating a scene that would have Rachel wringing a peal over her head for a sennight. Her gaze locked with his for a few moments more, brazening it out, before her eyes shifted nervously back to the fish on her plate.

She waited until Lord Rule had resumed his meal before speaking again. Just as he had deposited a medium-sized bite of succulent fish in his mouth she shared a bit of unusual knowledge with the rest of the company. "Did you know that many tradesmen inflate their meat—and most especially their *fish*—by having gin drinkers blow into the bodies? Indeed, and much of the seafood and meat that reaches our tables looking so thick and juicy has been made that way by having the poor animals heated or beaten while *still alive* in order to swell the meat. Isn't that interesting?"

The meal ended shortly after that, as the rest of the diners had somehow lost their appetites (indeed, Dexter, who had fled abruptly from the table, lost even more than that), which, while the thought of ruining Lucy's dinner party sat heavily on her mind, did at least serve one of the ends Mary had intended—getting herself shed of Tristan Rule's embarrassing presence before he drove her into strong hysterics.

Rachel had said he was a hot-tempered sort, prone to short, violent explosions of wrath. Putting all her eggs in one basket at the dinner table in hopes of having the man lose his composure, and therefore some of the esteem in which it seemed the rest of the company held him, had been the second reason for her outburst, but Rule had failed to perform according to his reputation, so that the affair had concluded with

Mary being the one who now sat in the corner of the Ruffton carriage in disgrace.

"Really, Mary, that was very poor-spirited of you," Rachel Gladwin was saying, for at least the third time in as many minutes. It took a lot to discompose Rachel—considering she had served as Lucy's companion during that trying time when the girl was so obviously pursuing an obviously fleeing Lord Thorpe—but Mary's inelegant observations at the dinner party had done it.

"I know, Aunt," Mary agreed sadly. "I promise to apologize to Lucy and Julian again when we reach the ball. I'll even send round a written apology tomorrow. But I was sorely tried, I tell you. If you had any idea what that odious nephew of yours had the nerve to intimate to me—"

Rachel could see Mary's blush even in the dim light cast by the flambeaux hung outside the carriage. "I'm listening," she nudged, remembering the smug look Tristan had been wearing as he and Dexter took their leave.

Mary gave a weak chuckle. "You may listen all you want, Aunt. His words were unrepeatable. I won't so demean myself as to quote the scoundrel."

Now it was Rachel's turn to smile. "Bested you, did he, little girl? I begin to scent a romance here myself. Won't Sir Henry be pleased?"

From the corner of the carriage came the unmistakable sound of fragile ivory fan sticks being snapped neatly in two.

Mary had just begun to relax when Tristan Rule and his ever-present shadow, Dexter, entered the Salerton ballroom and took up positions at the edge of the dance floor. He's playing me like a fish on a line, Mary fumed silently as she went down the dance with her latest partner. Ever since he first sank his hook into me he's been feeding me more and more line, making me believe I'm about to gain my freedom, and then, just when I'm feeling secure, yanking hard on the pole again.

As she whirled and dipped, flirting outrageously with the hapless young swain who had nearly tripped into a potted palm at the edge of the floor when Mary flashed him her brightest smile, she kept one eye firmly on the black-clad figure who looked as if he was about to spring on her even as he relaxed one well-defined shoulder against a marble pillar.

She never remembered what she said to her partner as he escorted her back to her aunt at the conclusion of the set, but if the youth's bemused expression was to be believed, her vague response to his parting question just might have gained Sir Henry yet another application for her hand on the morrow. Mary frowned, for she was not really heartless and had certainly not meant to lead Lord Hawlsey on, but then, as the musicians struck up the new, daring waltz, all thoughts of Lord Hawlsey fled as her spine automatically stiffened when she felt rather than heard Lord Rule's approach.

Bowing in front of Rachel for her permission— a curiously tunnel-sighted Rachel who seemed not to see her charge's frantic signal in the negative—Tristan availed himself of Mary's small hand and led her firmly onto the floor.

Lord Petersham always wore brown, Mary thought spitefully, and only succeeded in looking dashed dull. Then there was that silly man who wore nothing but green, like some sort of living plant. It stood to reason that Tristan Rule, who dressed only in funereal black, should look dull, or silly, or boringly unimaginative, or, at the very least, depressing. So why did he look none of these? Why did he look like his muscular torso had been carefully poured into his formfitting coat, his, in this instance, black satin breeches lovingly painted on? Why did his black-on-black embroidered waistcoat call such unladylike attention to his flat abdomen, his snowy cravat show to such advantage against his deeply tanned features, his equally white stockings delineate muscular calves that owed nothing to the sawdust stuffing so many men felt forced to use to supplement what nature and a sybaritic life had left lacking?

"I'm waiting, Miss Lawrence."

The sound of Lord Rule's low, husky voice jolted Mary from her musings and surprised her into looking directly into a pair of the deepest, darkest eyes she had ever seen. "W-waiting, my lord?" she stammered, irritated for allowing a tremor to slip into her voice. "Whatever for?"

Tristan cocked his dark head slightly to one side. "Why, for you to commence flirting with me, what else? You flirt with every man you dance with—every man save me, that is. After weeks of standing up with you only to have to propel you woodenly, and silently, round yet another endless ballroom, I have decided to take the initiative. Please, feel free to bat those outrageous eyelashes at me. I'm stronger than I look, I can take it."

Mary nearly tripped over her own feet as she stood stock-still for a moment, in mingled shock and outrage, while Tristan kept on dancing without missing a beat. "Me? *Talk* to you—the Great Sphinx? *Flirt* with you—the Great Stone Man? Why should I so lower myself as to try to converse with you when you've never so much as asked me if I thought the weather was tolerably fine? Besides, I'd rather flirt with porty old Prinny than waste even a moment's time searching my brain for anything civil I'd wish to say to you."

Believing she had succeeded in making her position crystal clear, Mary lowered her head and went back to staring a hole in his cravat.

"You can't flirt with pudgy old Prinny, Miss Lawrence," Tristan returned conversationally, "unless, of course, you wish to incur the wrath of the pudgy old Marchioness of Hertford, who is our Royal Highness's current favorite. In any event, the Regent is otherwise engaged these days, with he and his brother, the Duke of York, indulging once more in their favorite pastime, drinking each other under the table. Pity, though," he ended facetiously, "as I do believe it would be a sight not to be missed."

Feeling the heat of his left hand through her gloved fingers while sensing the steel in the hand that held her waist so firmly, Mary fought the urge to break away from the man, knowing that he was just obstinate enough to refuse to let her go—causing a scene of no mean proportions right in the middle of the ball. "Why, my lord," she settled for saying, "I do believe your cousins to be entirely wrong about you. They have hinted on more than one occasion that you were a secret, valuable tool of England's war effort. Wouldn't they be crushed to learn that in reality you are nothing more than a spiteful, gossipy old woman?"

A slight tick appeared along one side of Lord Rule's finely chiseled square chin, but he refused to allow this infuriating chit to bait him into unleashing his legendary temper. Let her continue to believe he was harmless, it would be easier to learn what he had set himself to discover if she continued to underestimate him. "Ah, Miss Lawrence," he returned, smiling, "you have found me out. But then, what else is there to do now that peace is here but tear up our contemporaries behind their backs? It is a prerequisite of anyone claiming to be of the British upper class."

"Bah? You British—" Mary began, then just as quickly ended. "You British men are all alike. You make a vocation out of refusing to take anything seriously. Why, Sir Henry has even said that English lords go to war with much the same enthusiasm as they approach grouse hunting, except that they don't tend to regard war quite so seriously."

The waltz ended, and Tristan put a hand under Mary's elbow and steered her toward a door to the first-floor balcony without her ever realizing their destination. "Sir Henry is absolutely correct, Miss Lawrence," he supplied smoothly as he helped her over the raised threshold and out onto the flagstones. "I've heard it more than once that we English believe all foreigners to be deucedly poor shots. Yet, be that as it may, we vain, arrogant English *have* succeeded in winning the war."

"Have we?" Mary countered, seating herself on a low stone bench and watching as Tristan eased himself down beside her. "My uncle mutters that the only change thus far in Paris is that the newspapers and pats of butter are now imprinted with *fleur-de-lis*."

Tristan berated himself for noticing how intriguingly Mary's clear complexion captured the moonlight and added, "But that is not the worst that is being said, Miss Lawrence. Although I cannot claim to know anything about it, I have heard that it was English money used to bribe Napoleon's generals that won us this war, just as it has done down through history, and that, in truth, Napoleon is very much Wellington's superior."

"As they have not faced each other across a battlefield, I believe that last to be a moot point, my lord," Mary replied, wondering why her answer had brought a thoughtful frown to Lord Rule's face.

"Then you have no preference between

Napoleon and the duke? Surely you must have an opinion?'' Tristan pressed.

"I must?" Mary shot back, suddenly realizing that she had somehow allowed herself to be isolated with a man she thoroughly detested. "Why? Surely a woman is not expected to have a head for war or politics. All that concerns me is that we are now free to visit Paris and investigate all the latest fashions."

"And yet you are still here in London," he pointed out, much to her chagrin. "I find it hard to believe you were not off to the Continent the minute Napoleon's abdication was declared."

This subject was close enough to Mary's heart to cloud her earlier suspicions. "And I would have been, if not for Sir Henry's summons," she blurted before getting a belated hold on her tongue. Why was she feeling like a butterfly pinned down to a table for examination? Why did this seemingly innocent conversation seem so contrived, so full of probing questions? Why was she sitting here in the moonlight with a man she thoroughly abhorred in the first place? Rising to her feet with more haste than grace, she told Tristan that she had been absent too long from the ballroom and must return.

Tristan rose with her, once more taking firm possession of her elbow. "We wouldn't want the tongues to wag, now would we, Miss Lawrence?" he agreed, just as if she had voiced the notion that the two of them were becoming thought of as a couple. "Besides, I do believe I heard another waltz beginning. I should be pleased to partner you."

That stopped Mary in her tracks. Wheeling to face him, she gritted, "Are you mad? *Two* waltzes? Add that to our disappearance from the room and the whole world will have us betrothed."

Tristan, who had decided to intensify his

campaign with Mary by sticking as close as a barnacle to her side until he made up his mind about her once and for all, only smiled—causing Mary's hand to itch to slap his handsome face. "Yes, they would, wouldn't they? Ah well, I daresay Sir Henry won't mind—he's always seemed to like me a bit. Do you wish a long engagement?"

CHAPTER THREE

Listening to Tristan's words, then whirling about to look into his disgustingly handsome, smiling face, caused Mary to spend the last coin of her self-control. "Marry you!" she shrieked, causing more than one interested head to turn in her direction. "Why, I'd rather be the sole woman on an island inhabited by shipwrecked sailors!"

Rule barely stifled an appreciative smile, which only served to incense Mary all the more, and bowed deeply from his waist. "And here I thought we were getting along so well," he said, making a poor attempt at looking crushed by her words. "I stand corrected, madam."

"Only until I knock you down, sirrah!" Mary retorted, trying to disengage her elbow, which he had maddeningly taken in his grasp. "Which I promise you I shall do shortly, if you do not release me."

Any lingering trace of humor left Lord Rule's face as he, by the simple means of closing his strong fingers around Mary's tender elbow, steered her over to a secluded corner of the balcony and lowered his head to within scant inches of hers. "What kind of woman are you?" he demanded harshly, giving her abused arm a shake. "I try to be civil to you, even flatter you by indulging in a bit of mild flirtation such as you

35

females demand of us men, and you repay me time after time with cutting words, insults, and now threats of violence.''

"Flirt with me! You call your outrageous suggestion *flirting*? And what do you mean by lumping me in with a bunch of chits with more hair than wit who giggle and simper as some ridiculous fop or other compares their crossed eyes to brightly shining stars?'' Mary was so angry now that she either could not or would not take notice of his lordship's set jaw and narrowed eyes. Raising her chin just a bit more, she sniffed dismissingly. "If you are going to ape your betters, I suggest you chose your models with more care.''

She was going to drive him straight out of his mind! His short-lived idea of insinuating himself into her good graces (all the better to keep a close watch on her) died an undignified death as his quick temper overrode his seldom-exercised discretion. Tristan stepped further back into the shadows, pulling Mary along with him willy-nilly, and took the back of her neck in his firm grip. "I am done playing games with you, Miss Lawrence. You tell me I am no gentleman, yet I have only your word for it that you are a lady.''

Mary's heart began to pound as she belatedly realized that her sharp tongue had gotten her into yet another tight spot. "Apply to my uncle if you wish a tracing of my family tree.'' She brazened it out, her green eyes spitting fire in the darkness. "I am not about to justify my existence to you.''

"I have talked with Sir Henry,'' Tristan informed her to her dismay, "and all he says is that you are the daughter of an old friend. You have the man so besotted he'll say anything to protect you, but I am not so hoodwinked by your beauty that I can overlook the fact that you have somehow established yourself in the house of one of the most important men in the war effort.''

Even in the midst of her fright Mary took a small bit of satisfaction in the notion that Lord Rule thought her beautiful, but that admission did not serve to overshadow the fact that he was accusing her of—what *was* he accusing her of? "You think I'm sir Henry's *mistress?*" she squeaked at last, feeling something akin to relief.

Tristan's fingers tightened on the soft, slim neck. "Mistress?" he repeated, brought up short. "No, Rachel wouldn't stand still for being a party to that, not even for an old friend . . . would she?" he questioned softly, as if debating with himself.

Mary reached up and tried to remove his hand, finger by tensed finger. "Look, my lord, either throttle me or let me go. Make up your mind." In the space of a moment she had decided that Tristan Rule was not ruthless—he was ridiculous! But if he was suffering from overexposure to battle or some such thing, he should take himself off to some spa for the waters, not run amok in London searching out nonexistent intrigues. Besides, she reminded herself as she attempted to lift his thumb from the pulse point at the base of her throat, it wasn't as if there was no intrigue about her presence in Sir Henry's household— even though her true identity was not all that earthshaking. The last thing her uncle would wish for was this man meddling in their affairs.

Lord Rule shook his head a time or two, bringing himself back to the matter at hand. And that matter was, to be obvious about the thing, that the matter at hand *was* his hand—for somehow it had found its way around Miss Lawrence's slender throat. God! The woman had the power to drive him distracted. And the thought that she could be Sir Henry's mistress did something evil to his insides that he was powerless to deny. Looking down into her angry face, Tristan cudgeled his brain for a way out of this latest coil into which the dratted chit had succeeded in goading him.

"Well sir," Mary prompted, puzzled by the slightly dazed expression in Lord Rule's dark eyes. "Which is it to be—a quick snuffing or sweet freedom?"

What would Julian do in a situation like this? Or Kit? Tristan cursed under his breath as he realized neither of those esteemed gentlemen would have allowed themselves to be drawn into such a tangled mess in the first place. But then neither of those men had ever stood within a heartbeat of the beautiful, willful, mysterious Miss Mary Lawrence. Any man could be excused for losing his head in such circumstances, he assured himself, regaining a small bit of his consequence while fueling his flagging temper with yet another shovelful of Mary Lawrence's supposed sins against him.

The firm clasp turned abruptly into a rough sort of caress as Tristan Rule smiled evilly, and Mary found herself wishing he were still scowling. "Wh-what are you going to do?" she asked, already knowing the answer.

"What do you think I'm going to do?" Tristan returned in a soft growl. If he was already in trouble—and he knew he most assuredly would be the moment Sir Henry heard of this night's work —he'd already decided he may as well be hung for a sheep as a lamb. His dark features nearly blotting out the moonlight as they descended on her, Tristan ended huskily, "I'm going to throttle you, what else?"

"No!" Mary protested swiftly, but not nearly quickly enough to keep her denial from being smothered by Lord Rule's punishing mouth. Nor did her hands move rapidly enough to prevent his arms from capturing her slim body in his rock-hard embrace.

Mary had been kissed before, she was sure she had, but all of those kisses paled beneath the reality of Tristan's mouth as it curved, and slanted, and moved possessively upon hers. As his strong arms forced the very air from her lungs, he captured her breath in his mouth and breathed his own life back into her. It was so personal, so intimate an action, that she felt herself to have been actually violated. When the tip of his tongue slid along the edge of her teeth as his mouth opened more fully over hers, then brazenly penetrated, Mary instinctively fought back.

"*Ouch!* You hellion!" Tristan spat, jumping back to reach a finger inside his mouth to inspect his wounded tongue.

Her hands balled into fists at her sides, her firm chin outthrust in indignation, Mary warned coldly: "Touch me again, you miserable creature —even come within a mile of me—and I'll have you horsewhipped!"

Watching appreciatively as Mary's indignant figure stomped back into the ballroom, his hand held to the cheek she had slapped with some force in order to punctuate her parting warning, Tristan mused aloud, "She'd probably do it too. And at the moment, by God, it almost seems worth it."

Rachel had observed Mary's departure with Rule, and had counted the minutes until her charge had returned alone to the ballroom, looking more than a little the worse for wear. But before Rachel could cross the floor to find out just what her infuriating nephew had done this time, Mary was claimed for a dance by some violet satin-clad exquisite and disappeared into the crowd of revelers.

That left Tristan, and Rachel was determined not to let the fellow get away without an explanation of what had transpired on the balcony. She found him lounging against the doorjamb, boring a hole in Mary's unsuspecting back like some hot-headed halfling. She looked from Tristan to Mary and then back again, hardly believing what her eyes were telling her. It couldn't be. It was utterly impossible. The Ruthless Lord Rule pricked by Cupid's dart? Tristan was just shy of his thirtieth birthday, and in all that time he had never once shown any signs of being the romantic sort. True, she owned to herself, he had been hopping about the Continent and God only knew where else these past seven years or more, but considering the multitude of rumors about his involvement with the military, it seemed impossible for him to have carried on any serious romantic interlude without all of London finding out about it one way or another.

Tilting her head to one side, she inspected Tristan's expression as he stood rock still, his whole body taut with suppressed—what? Fury? Passion? Lust? "Good heavens," she whispered, "this novel writing has made me into a hysteric. Soon I'll be reading Byron and swooning dead away." Still, she thought as she looked at her nephew again, more objectively this time, Rule does have a certain look about him—the same sort of look, if I recall it correctly, that he had at the age of twelve, when his father refused to allow him on that great big stallion. And when Rachel recalled that Tristan had eventually not only mounted that stallion, but broken him to saddle, her fears for her charge began anew.

"Tristan," she said, tugging on his sleeve to get his attention, "you look like a thundercloud. Kindly smile at me as if you didn't wish me at the farthest corners of the earth and stop casting a pall over this entire company. I swear three totally innocent gentlemen have already departed the ballroom, believing you had them in their sights."

Distracted, Rule ignored his aunt's sarcasm, if indeed he had understood it. After all, he wasn't deliberately striking a pose or any such thing. He was merely being himself—his intense, determined, passionate self. He might, in his more candid moments, admit to possessing a bit of a short fuse, but he consoled himself with the knowledge that he was never purposely mean. He leveled one long, last piercing look at the scrap of female that could just be the exception to his self-imposed rule of absolute chivalry where the weaker sex was concerned, and turned to address his aunt. "You wanted something, Aunt? A cooling glass of lemonade, perhaps?"

Rachel clenched her teeth in frustration. Tristan had always had this maddening ability to turn her up sweet just when she was about to tear a wide strip off his hide. A glass of lemonade, indeed! Better to have three fingers of whiskey if she was about to try to beat some sense into the idiot's thick head! "No, thank you, dear," she somehow trilled, taking his arm. "But it is dreadfully close in the ballroom. Perhaps you could bear me company for a stroll around the balcony?"

Again Tristan looked to the dance floor, where Mary was busily flirting with three gentlemen who were all vying for her hand for the next set, and then back at his aunt. "A stroll, you say? On the balcony? Couldn't you just stand here in the doorway and take a few deep, bracing breaths?"

"Tristan Montgomery Rule!" Rachel snapped, longing to do him an injury. "Come with me willingly or I'll pull you along by the ear like I did when you were in short pants!" And with that, she sailed off through the archway—her reluctant nephew trailing along behind—and prepared to bribe, bluster, threaten, or cajole the truth out of him. She owed it to Henry!

* * *

" 'Ere now, are yer gonna eat wit dem dabblers on?" Ben questioned Mary, who had yet to relinquish her gloves into the servant's waiting hands. "Yer be 'ere fer yafflin' ain't yer? Montague's done up a treat, so's yer best be clammed."

Mary turned to her aunt. "What did he say?" she asked, prudently giving over her gloves before the little fellow stripped them from her hands. "And what's a Montague?"

Rachel nodded to the now deeply bowing Ben and propelled her charge up the stairs to the drawing room where Jennie and Lucy waited. "Montague is Jennie's idea of a French chef, and you'd better be hungry or there may be the devil to pay. It's a long story," she conceded as Mary's mouth opened on another question. "Suffice it to say Jennie has these little *projects*. For the moment, my dear, just follow my lead." They stopped before the drawing-room door so that Ben could dash by and announce them, muttering something about earning his pantler's keys (butler's keys, to the uninformed, which Rachel, to her own regret, had not been ever since her chaperonage of Lucy). After allowing themselves to be trumpeted into the room like minor royalty, Rachel called the three young women quickly to order.

"I know it is my custom to retire to a corner and let you girls natter as you will, but I have requested this luncheon with a definite purpose in mind," she began, quickly taking Jennie and Lucy's interest away from Mary's fetching new walking dress and onto herself.

"What ho? Do I sense some deep intrigue?" Lucy asked happily, clapping her hands.

"You *always* sense some deep intrigue," Jennie commented to Lucy without rancor before turning back to her aunt. "Has someone unsuitable offered for Mary?" she asked, her thoughts, as usual, running along matrimonial lines.

"Is Uncle Henry at last agreed to send me to France?" Mary chimed in, immediately crossing her fingers for luck.

"Perhaps, no, and no, *definitely* not," Rachel replied, pointing to each of the trio of young hopefuls in turn. "This meeting concerns one Tristan Rule. Something has got to be done about the boy."

"Marry him off!" Lucy and Jennie declared in unison, while Mary's only reply was to pucker up her nose in an expression of distaste, saying, "And a more boring subject I cannot imagine."

Rachel sat down gingerly on the edge of the satin settee and addressed her next words directly to Mary. "You won't believe it boring when I have told you just what maggot my nephew has taken into his head about you. I don't remember him going off on such a wild tangent since that time he decided Lucy was really a boy in disguise and her father had put her into skirts so that he wouldn't have to spring for an education at Eton."

Jennie whirled on Lucy, who was laughing uproariously. "Lucy!" she exclaimed. "He never did! How old was Tristan when this happened?"

Lucy had to take refuge in her handkerchief as tears of mirth streamed from her eyes. "T-ten!" she chortled. "I was just a little past three myself. Oh dear, you would perish on the spot if I told you how Tristan was at last proved wrong. Thank goodness I have little but a hazy remembrance of his triumphant unveiling of my 'masculine' form in front of the vicar and his sister. I swear, Tristan couldn't sit down for a week after my father got through with him!"

Mary found herself laughing in spite of herself,

and in spite of the deep animosity she felt for
Tristan Rule—especially after the events of the
previous evening. The fact that she knew she
couldn't confide in either Rachel or Sir Henry
without somewhat incriminating herself for her
own less than ladylike behavior did not detract
from the poor opinion of the man. Trying to keep
her mind on the subject at hand, she put in, "I
gather, Aunt, that your nephew's latest incorrect
assumption is even worse?"

There was no way to dress the thing up in fine
linen, and Rachel was not about to try. Taking a
deep, steadying breath, she announced baldly:
"Tristan believes Mary might be a spy in the pay of
Napoleon."

Looking quite clearly puzzled, Jennie murmured, "But Napoleon is imprisoned on Elba. The
war is *over*. Surely Kit would have told me if there
was any danger. We plan to travel there next
spring with Christopher and my father. And
Montague was so looking forward to it too—he's
French, you know."

Rachel shook her head. "*We* consider the war to
be over, pet, but even Sir Henry is uneasy about
the laxity of Bonaparte's imprisonment. There has
been more than one rumor about forces being at
work to reinstate the man in Paris. He still carries
the title of emperor, you know, even if he is in
exile."

While Rachel was explaining all this to Jennie,
Lucy was observing Mary shrewdly out of the
corners of her eyes. The girl was sitting as stiff
and still as a ramrod, looking as if steam would
commence pouring from her ears at any moment.
Obviously Mary did not share Rachel's apprehension, Jennie's confusion, or her own hilarity—no,
Miss Mary Lawrence was, in a word, *incensed*!

"How dare he," Mary whispered nearly under

her breath, and then more loudly. "How *dare* he!"

Immediately Jennie set out to placate her guest. "Now, Mary, don't be so out-of-reason cross. Tristan has simply made an error in judgment. Surely Aunt Rachel has already set him straight."

"It's not for myself that I'm angry, Jennie," Mary explained, rising to her feet to begin pacing up and down the length of the carpet. "It's the insult to Sir Henry that I cannot and will not abide! How *dare* that ridiculous man cast such aspersions on the intelligence and discretion of one of the nation's greatest patriots? For myself I care nothing, for Tristan Rule's opinion of me is not something I would lose any sleep over, I assure you, but if Sir Henry were to catch wind of this—why, I cannot imagine the consequences."

Rachel could. Rachel had. Which was why she was sitting here amid a group of painfully young ladies instead of pouring out her fears to the one man who she felt could settle the matter once and for all. Oh yes, she had thought of confiding in Julian or Kit, but since it was so pleasant to have her two nieces so happily married, she should hate having to start over from scratch finding replacements once that hotheaded Tristan had made them both into widows. Especially Lucy—dear Lord, getting that one bracketed had cost Rachel more than a few gray hairs!

"I have, unlike you, had a full night to ponder our problem, so I have entertained a few ideas ..." Rachel slid in before Mary could snatch up her reticule and go off searching for Lord Rule in order to bash him soundly about the head and shoulders. All three pairs of young eyes immediately concentrated in her direction.

Agreeing with Mary that Sir Henry was best left ignorant of Rule's assumption, Rachel admitted that the only concrete idea she could come up with was that Tristan Rule needed to be taught a lesson —a very strong lesson. She was now, she told them sincerely, applying to three of the most agile, devious, determined minds she knew for ways to render to her nephew the trimming he so obviously deserved.

"We could have him impressed in His Majesty's service on a ship bound for deepest Africa," Mary offered most evilly.

Rachel declined that option, warning, "Mary, my dear, if you would please try for a little more elegance of mind? Besides, knowing Tristan, he would incite a mutiny within three days of leaving port and return here with a full crew of faithful sailors bound to help him expose your dastardly purpose. No, much as I wish it, we shall have to *deal* with Tristan, not merely transport him."

Mary just shrugged, then suggested a second option—something vaguely connected with boiling his lordship in oil.

"Oh, I do like this girl!" Lucy said, giggling. "No simpering miss, this."

Slowly it dawned on the company that Jennie had not spoken for some time. Lucy looked over at her cousin to find the girl wiping away a tear, and promptly asked her what was amiss. "I've been thinking about poor Mary, and how she must feel to be supposed guilty of such a grievous crime," Jennie supplied before daintily blowing her nose. "It is horrid, simply horrid! I wonder how Tristan would feel to be placed in such a position. Perhaps if the slipper were on the other foot for a change, it might show him how unfair his assumptions can be."

Mary immediately stopped her pacing, an unholy grin lighting her beautiful face. Racing over to swoop the still-sniffling Jennie into her arms, she gave that girl a resounding kiss on the cheek. "Jennie, you dearest thing, you have hit upon it exactly. Lord Rule is long overdue for a lesson. For too long has he been allowed to make hare-witted assumptions about his fellow man and then set about proving how right he is, no matter what the cost to his victim. For Lucy's injured sensibilities as a child, for his insult to Sir Henry, and for all the other people he has persecuted with his single-minded, not to mention simpleminded determination—*we shall teach him a lesson*!"

Lucy tipped her head to one side. "I agree about the rest of it, but I don't know if you can truthfully say I was a victim," she corrected impishly. "After all, I have it from my old nurse that I quite enjoyed showing off for the vicar, and repeated the practice every time an adult came into range for the next few months—until Papa finally broke me of the habit."

"How did he do that?" Jennie was the only person interested enough to inquire.

"By the simple expedient of basting her drawers to her shift until she got the message," Rachel supplied, smiling a bit to herself. "It was my idea, actually. Hale wrote to me in desperation."

Ben entered the room and announced luncheon with all the pomp and ceremony Montague's creations deserved, and Jennie quickly ushered her guests into the dining room, where Mary once again commanded everyone's attention by unveiling the plan that had already grown to major proportions within her agile brain. If Tristan Rule had thought he could prove Mary to be a spy, she was going to be extremely helpful in convincing him of her guilt! In other words, if he wished her to act like a traitor, she would accommodate him—in spades.

"Oh, for a humdrum existence," Rachel said to no one in particular, envying every bored on-the-shelf spinster in all England.

Lucy was all for Mary's idea. Indeed, she even

volunteered her every assistance, but she couldn't help but ask: "Just how is this going to provide Tris with his overdue lesson in minding his own business? I mean, skulking about leaving messages and acting suspicious sounds like whacking great fun, but surely it will only work to make Tristan more sure of his convictions."

"Not if I—with a little help from you, my dear friends—also behave as if Tristan is the *real* French spy in our midst, and return his treatment of me twofold!" Mary told them confidently.

Lifting her glass in a salute to her new friend's genius, Lucy promised jovially, "And when it is all over, and Tristan has been suitably humbled, he will fall at your feet begging for your hand in marriage!"

Mary's smile faded as she remembered the events of the previous evening. "Then I will have him aboard that ship to Africa after all!" she vowed sincerely, not noticing Jennie's and Lucy's exchange of broad winks.

CHAPTER FOUR

Mary flung down the magazine she had been reading, unable to sustain an interest in a gushing description of the latest fashions from Paris, and hopped up to pace back and forth impatiently across the drawing-room rug, her small hands clenched into unladylike fists. Oh, she was so angry! Drat that Tristan Rule anyway!

She halted in her tracks momentarily to stare malevolently at a Sevres figurine, seeing Rule's dark, well-made features rather than the smiling face of an innocent young country maid dressed in pink ruffles. Who does he think he is, she ranted to herself, to be judging me like the Lord on Doomsday? He's an obtuse, despicable, intolerable, opinionated . . . Mary turned on her heels and set about pacing once more, unable to continue her thoughts else she'd be forced to throw something.

And it wasn't bad enough that the man had all but convicted her of spying for the French, oh no— he had also shown her, by his actions of the previous week, that he was not about to do his accusing from the sidelines. Acting as if she had never warned him to approach her again, he had been up to his old tricks, standing up with her for the length of one infuriating dance and then retiring to a nearby pillar to glower at her like some angry ancient god for the remainder of the evening, just as if he expected her to give herself away somehow, proving his ludicrous theory to be correct.

Even worse, everyone was so all-fired afraid of the man. It was almost ridiculous to see all her former beaux defecting from the ranks one by one as they put their tails between their legs and ran from Rule's intense stares. How was she to have any fun at all if her main amusement—harmless flirting—was to be denied her? What it had come to, she realized as she brought herself up with a start, was that she had only two options open to her—either allowing Rule to court her openly so that she could at least go out in society without feeling like a pariah, or else retiring posthaste to a nunnery!

Crash! It was no use—something had to satisfy Mary's outrage, and the china maiden had been elected. Staring at the porcelain shards scattered about in the cold fireplace, Mary was angered even more when she realized that she had broken a valuable piece of Sir Henry's property without the action easing her fury by so much as a jot. Oh, if only she could have Rule here in person; smashing *him* would be entire worlds more satisfying.

Almost as if she had conjured him up by sheer force of will, she whirled at the sound of the butler's announcement to see Tristan Rule striding big as life into the drawing room. "You!" she exclaimed, her eyes narrowing dangerously. "What do you want?"

Tristan quickly took in Mary's flushed cheeks and belligerent stance and impulsively decided to change his mission from that of seeing his aunt to the possibly more profitable one of trying to goad Mary Lawrence into betraying her guilt. "*Bonjour, mademoiselle,*" he pronounced in perfect accents, making her an elegant leg.

"It was," Mary snapped peevishly, and then,

sparked by an imp of perversity that she could no more deny than she could her need to breathe, she launched herself into a long, involved speech concerning the growing list of fêtes and receptions planned for the upcoming celebration of peace, all in faultless French. There! If the man wants signs of guilt, I'll give him signs of guilt until he drowns himself in them!

Tristan could not hide his triumphant smile. The chit spoke French like a native of that country. Even he, trained in several languages, could find nothing to fault in her accent or usage. "Your French tutor must have been an émigré, Miss Lawrence, to have taught you so well," he offered as bait.

Mary opened her mouth as if to speak, then lifted an anxious hand to her breast and stammered nervously, "Y-yes, yes *indeed*. How clever of you. That's *precisely* who it was. A poor émigré. The wretched creature so needed employment at the time that I ended up having a resident tutor for several years whilst I was in Sussex." There, she thought, hiding a grin. That should serve to convince him I'm lying through my teeth. Ah, look at him, smiling one of his devilish secretive smiles, just like the cat who got into the cream. I'm surprised he hasn't already sent for the constable, so sure of himself is he.

"Tristan! What brings you here today? And Mary, why didn't you have me summoned at once? You know you should not be entertaining a gentleman without a chaperon."

"Was I?" Mary commented under her breath as she looked apologetically at her companion.

Rachel's entrance into the room startled Rule into looking up blankly for a moment, and Rachel heaved a small sigh of relief when she realized that her nephew and Mary hadn't come to fisticuffs before she could place herself as a buffer between their two warlike personalities. "Have you come to see Sir Henry, nephew? He is out at present, but we expect him back directly."

"He is back," came Sir Henry's voice, shortly to be followed by that man's pudgy presence in the doorway. "Come courting, have you, boy? Since I saw you not an hour ago at the War Office, it can't be my face you were longing to see." Sir Henry nodded his head a time or two, a broad smile on his cherubic face. "Good, good. I rather like the idea of Tristan running tame in his house, Rachel. He's a hotheaded young puppy, but loyal as the day is long, and valuable. You couldn't make a better choice, Mary, my dear, not if you looked for a dozen Seasons. Right, Rachel?"

Rachel closed her eyes and shook her head, not knowing whether to box Sir Henry's ears or give him a smacking great kiss on the mouth. But one way or another—due to his foolish blustering—matters were about to come to a head, and Rachel couldn't be happier. All this scheming and plotting among Mary and her two nieces on the one side and Tristan, aided by his fertile imagination and stubborn tenacity, on the other was sure to lead her to an early grave—and with her novel just begun. At least now either Mary or Tristan, or both of them, would be forced to own to the truth before Sir Henry went posting the banns.

Tristan, however, was not about to look what he saw as a gift horse in the molars. Instead of denying that he was indeed love-bitten, or even running from the house and matrimony in full bachelor flight, he was saying something ridiculously silly about wishing to take the charming Miss Lawrence for a ride in the promenade in order to convince her that he was sincere in his regard for her.

Clearly, Tristan had twisted everything round to his own advantage and could care less what Sir Henry supposed as long as he could proceed unimpeded in his quest to have Mary to himself in order to ascertain once and for all whether or not she was a traitor.

That left Mary, and Rachel turned to look at her appealingly, hoping that the child had reconsidered her plans now that Sir Henry could end up the innocent victim in the affair. But if sane, rational thinking in the face of impending disaster was what Rachel had hoped for, she was due for a disappointment that would keep her up nights for a long time to come.

Mary, hiding her furiously clenched fists behind her back, was just then smiling sweetly and denying nothing. Indeed, she was looking up into Tristan's handsome features with a look so cloyingly sweet that Rachel knew she, for one, would be put off sugaring her tea for a sennight.

Tilting her head slightly to one side in a move meant to be coquettish, Mary blushed becomingly (a trick she had mastered in her cot) and simpered, "Oh, Sir Henry! Do you think I *should*? After the marked attentions Lord Rule has been so kind as to show me, I scarce wish the vulgar tattles to have more to prattle about." She then hesitated, overdoing things a little bit, Rachel thought, by putting her fingers to her mouth and giggling, before admitting, "But I would like to ride up beside Lord Rule above *all things*!"

"I'll have your maid bring your cloak and bonnet, Mary," Rachel volunteered from between clenched teeth, frantic to quit the room before she did either her overacting charge or her sleuthing nephew an injury.

Within ten minutes a beaming, benevolent Sir Henry and a resigned, realistic Rachel were standing at the front door, waving the young couple on their way.

By the time they arrived in the park, Mary's good humor had been much restored, thanks to the brilliant idea she'd had as she spied a rather down at the heels *frizeur*, hatbox in hand, crossing the street in front of them. Catching the Frenchman's attention by the simple expediency of a maidenly screech supposedly caused by the distressing sight of a rather large, slavering dog, Mary took great pains in gifting the hairdresser with a broad wink and a furtive-looking wave of the hand before hastily pretending an unnatural interest in one fingertip of her right glove.

It is superfluous to report that this supposedly covert signal was witnessed by the ever-alert Tristan, just as any of that man's enemies would be quick to point out to the assumed-to-be-careless Miss Lawrence.

Filing away a mental picture of the Frenchman before urging his team forward once more, Tristan determined to seek out Mary's "contact" and question him as soon as possible, a notion that Mary—just then snickering into her gloved hand—found distinctly amusing. Soon, with any luck at all, she'd have Tristan so busy chasing ridiculous false leads all over London that he wouldn't have a single moment left free to tease her with his unwanted attentions.

If she had any slight qualms about the course of action she had embarked upon since hearing of Tristan's assumptions about her, his earnest reaction to her pretended message-passing effectively banished the last of her more tender feelings.

But it would not do to have this thing all one-sided. As Jennie had said, it was time Tristan learned just how it felt to be pursued like some helpless deer hunted in a fenced wood. Yes, it was time she started giving him a hint or two about her own, deliberately amateurish investigation of *his* loyalties.

She began the moment Rule's curricle was eased into line behind a dowager countess's rusty black barouche, ready to take their part in the late-afternoon promenade. "You understood my French quite well, my lord," she began innocently enough. "Perhaps you too have a French émigré as a tutor?"

This seemingly artlessly posed query brought surprising results. Not accustomed to being questioned on his personal life, Rule answered her question with one of his own. "Why do you ask?" he shot back quickly.

Mary took refuge in another girlish giggle. Goodness, the man was touchy! "Lud, my lord," she needled him, "anyone would think you had learned your French at Boney's knee, for all you're so ticklish about the subject. I told you about *my* tutor; surely *your* knowledge of the language was not gained through some nefarious means, was it?"

What the deuce was the girl up to? Tristan pretended to concentrate on his horses while he cudgeled his brain for an answer. She was only playacting at being a brainless ninny; he was not so obtuse as to not see through her pretense, but he was at a loss as to why.

Besides, it was he who had questions that needed answering, not she. *She* was the one with no traceable background, just as if she had been hatched full-grown from an egg three months earlier. It was *she* who had installed herself snugly in Sir Henry's house, hoodwinking that poor, naive man with her deadly charms; *she* who could be anyone from Sir Henry's by-blow to Bonaparte's first cousin. *She* was the one who had some serious explaining to do, and he was not about to allow her to turn the tables on him and try to make *him* England's fiercest patriot, into a person of questionable allegiance.

Turning in his seat, the better to see her reaction to his words, Tristan smiled broadly, saying, "Why, Miss Lawrence, what an odd imagination you have. *Nefarious* French lessons? You didn't strike me as one of those females who's addicted to those novels full of dark danger and imperiled innocents adrift in a cruel world."

Mary dug her fingernails into her palms until she could control her urge to do Lord Rule an injury. Then, returning his smile just as brilliantly, she trilled, "But Lord Rule, your own aunt is penning just such a novel. Surely you must hold her in disgust if your opinion of her chosen medium is so very low?"

"My aunt is merely filling her time until Sir Henry wakes up and realizes he cannot risk losing Rachel a second time and makes her his wife. I'll not begrudge her this little hobby if it makes her happy," he ended, just as if he had anything at all to say about the running of Rachel's life.

Looking around at the greening landscape and seeing everything through a red haze of anger, Mary found herself amazed yet again at the maddening way Lord Rule had of putting everything and everybody into neat little boxes, then labeling them as he saw fit. It was as if he had inherited some of Jennie's matchmaking tendencies—his cousin's burning desire to settle everyone happily into perfectly fitting niches—and some of his cousin Lucy's single-minded determination in following through on any project once undertaken, no matter what the odds, as well as more than his fair share of Lucy's tendency to meddle in whatever she considered to be her business.

What Mary had yet to fully understand was that Tristan—being the male of the species and therefore more prone to looking upon his less desirable traits as sterling qualities—had grown into manhood with his determination hardening into firm, unwavering resolve, while his wish to settle people changed into managing interference and his natural curiosity about his fellowman twisted into suspicion and mistrust of those he could not neatly categorize. And all of this had happened because no one had ever yet had sufficient courage to tell him he was fast becoming an opinionated, arrogant, fire-breathing Don Quixote—out to right the world's wrongs as he was so clearly, in his own mind, called upon to do.

Having been deeply involved with the defense of his country for the past seven years, his talents (or failings, depending on whom you applied to for a judgment) had been honed and refined until he felt himself able to judge and mentally file away a man within mere minutes of making his acquaintance. He did not give any credence to hearsay or rumor —and paid only a little more attention to the official documents he was frequently provided with to use as a guide—choosing instead to make up his own mind in his own way. In this manner he had decided that, seeing that Lucy trusted Julian, the man was obviously innocent of any involvement with the death of a young woman who had claimed to be his discarded mistress.

Yet, perversely, he had decided that Mary Lawrence—vouched for by his trusted superior, Sir Henry—a girl of no background who had popped up in the household of the same so-important Sir Henry, was a very dangerous woman. The unnerving way his skin tightened at the mere sight of her; the tendency the hair at the back of his

head had of bristling—tingling his scalp—at the
sound of her unaffected laugh; the unnatural
talent she had for bewitching all who came within
her charmed circle; everything about Mary
Lawrence screamed out at him *danger—danger*.

Although he could not, if pressed, produce a
single damning piece of evidence to support his
theory, Rule stuck buckle and thong to his initial
conclusion—either in deference to his seldom-off-
target intuition or because of that inborn streak of
stubbornness, not even he was able to say. All he
knew was that in all his nine and twenty years of
living, he had never before experienced this sense
of very real personal danger that he felt every time
he encountered Mary Lawrence . . . every time he
stood up for the waltz with Mary Lawrence.

His life had for many years depended on his
ability to judge people, and Mary, even though she
was living under Sir Henry's protection, even
though she looked as innocent as a newborn lamb,
even though she was the most beautiful,
fascinating woman he had ever met, was a prime
suspect in the newly discovered plot to free
Bonaparte from Elba and return him to Paris as
emperor. Hadn't he suspected her from the
moment he had arrived back in London after Sir
Henry's summons only to see the girl already
entrenched in Sir Henry's own home? And now,
having decided for himself that he was correct in
his assumptions, he would not rest until he
uncovered her entire scheme and unmasked her
co-conspirators.

Tristan looked over at Mary again, pretending
an interest in a showy stallion just then being
edged along the path by his proud owner, and
experienced yet again the unnerving tingle that
her mere proximity to his person invariably
provoked. Guilty as sin, he assured himself yet
again, unswerving in his belief in his own

intuition—and, unbeknownst to him, demonstrating yet again his total ignorance of the body's power to recognize what the mind refuses to accept.

The silence that had descended upon the pair ever since Tristan's casual dismissal of Rachel's motives for penning a novel had not bothered them as long as they were each locked in their own private thoughts.

While Rule's mind had traveled yet again down the same narrow road—the one that ended with proof of Mary's guilt being irrefutably laid at her doorstep Mary had taken her mind down quite another path entirely, one strewn with roadblocks set up to catch the sleuthing Lord Rule unawares and send him spinning posthaste into a water-filled ditch.

The man was more than insufferable, she had decided, with those condescending remarks about his aunt just another example of his overweening arrogance—and he was fast becoming a menace.

Oh yes, she had seen the dashing young Hussar smile and begin to approach the curricle before realizing who she was sitting up beside and beating a hasty retreat lest he run the chance of getting on Ruthless Rule's wrong side. And she had fumed impotently when three other gentlemen, two on horseback and one out driving his purple-turbaned mama, had only waved to her furtively and then scurried away—the latter gentleman nearly toppling his mama from the squabs in his haste to be off.

Lepers have more human contact, Mary thought in disgust. What is it about this fellow that sends strong men racing for cover and makes young ladies feel faint and reach for their hartshorn? Yes, she owned reluctantly, he was handsome enough to cause any number of swoons, but so far she had not seen even one enterprising miss work up sufficient nerve to so much as flutter an eyelash in his direction.

Mary smiled to herself. I must be some sort of extraordinary being—not only am I able to sit up alongside this man without suffering a hint of the vapors, but I am totally unafraid of the man or his disgusting nickname. And that presents me with a puzzle: for either everyone else is overreacting to the man's reputation and ridiculous affectations of black clothing and blacker stares, or I am contemplating the greatest folly imaginable by plotting intrigues against the most dangerous man in all of England.

And so it was that, just as Tristan was covertly peeping at Mary to assure himself once more of her guilt, Mary was, in her turn, covertly peeping at him, guilt written all over her beautiful oval-shaped face. Tristan's normally severe expression hardened into a cold mask as Mary's creamy complexion heated to a fiery red, and the two broke eye contact self-consciously to concentrate on viewing the scenery with a thoroughness that would make anyone suppose they were considering redesigning the entire park.

Now the silence became noticeably uncomfortable for both parties. Tristan watched as Mary's gloved hands folded and unfolded nervously in her lap, and he experienced a rare feeling of compassion—which he quickly squelched. They were caught up in the heavy traffic of carriages and curricles, and would be for at least another half hour, and he was not about to let this golden opportunity escape him.

"Miss Lawrence," he began, surprised to hear a hint of tenderness in his voice, "have I told you that I have recently been across to Paris?"

"Have you?" Mary commented, pushing down

the urge to tell him he should have stayed there and spared London and herself his obnoxious presence. "I hear it is very gay. Sir Henry says we may travel there next spring, but I am hoping to convince him it is quite safe enough now to visit. After all, *everyone* is there."

Continuing to direct his attention to his team, which was still at a standstill behind the rusty black barouche, Rule prodded, "You have a strong desire to set foot on French soil, Miss Lawrence?"

"I have a strong desire to set foot in a French dress shop, sir," she replied frankly. "And to visit Versailles, and see all the places I have only been told about, and to be invited to one of the exclusive salons, and to have my hand kissed by a dashing Frenchman." She sighed. "I desire only what every young woman in England desires, my lord. What did *you* find to amuse you whilst in Paris? Gambling houses? Beautiful women? Intrigue?"

He almost believed her, but her question, that seemed so innocent, set his defenses at attention once again. "I was there on orders from my government, Miss Lawrence. I found nothing to admire in a country that waged such a costly war against our people."

"Oh, my lord, how rigid you are!" Mary exclaimed, momentarily forgetting the part she had decided to play. "Surely you cannot condemn an entire country, an entire people, for the ambitions of a few? Surely it is Bonaparte's thirst for power and territory that must be condemned, and not the people he ruled. After all, they suffered too. Why, look at that disastrous retreat from Moscow. I understand thousands of poor soldiers perished in the snows."

" 'From the sublime to the ridiculous is but a step,' " Rule quoted quietly.

"What?"

"Bonaparte made that remark just before he deserted his troops to run back to Paris and raise another army to replace the one he squandered so carelessly in Russia," Rule told her informatively.

"How would you know that?" Mary asked, much impressed in spite of herself. "Surely you would have had to have been there to—oh my, sir, I do believe I'm beginning to place a bit more credence in the rumors I have heard about your exploits as a master spy!"

Rule's dark eyes took on a shuttered look as he recalled his infiltration into the ranks of retreating soldiers, wearing a filthy, torn uniform, his bare feet wrapped in the bloody rags he had taken from a man who had no further need for them, and remembered again how Bonaparte, before stepping back inside his closed coach, had placed a reassuring hand on his shoulder and promised to see them all again in Paris. How he had hated that man for the way he had ridden off, leaving his army to grope along toward the border without his guidance or the inspiration of his leadership.

But Tristan had done his job, and had slipped back into the trees to where his horse was waiting to carry him to safety and the first of the many couriers who would pass on the valuable information he had gleaned during the weeks he had watched Bonaparte's invincible *grande armée* degenerate into the ragged band of disease-ridden unfortunates who could conquer everything but the wrath of the Russian winter.

"I'll say it again, my lord," Mary pressed as she could see that Rule had retreated into what seemed to be an unpleasant memory, "you must have been a very proficient spy, just as it has been hinted, to have gleaned such personal conversation. Now that we are at peace again, couldn't you please satisfy my curiosity by telling me exactly what it was that made you so valuable to Sir Henry?"

"I traveled," Rule said shortly. "And I reported on what I saw. Nothing more."

"You traveled a war-torn contininent, my lord," Mary pointed out, knowing she was pushing the point. "You must have been in constant peril. Yet your reputation is for being ruthless, if I may be so bold as to point that out to you. Surely a mere informant would not earn such a title?"

Rule smiled at her, giving her credit for having the courage to put into words what other people— even his two audacious cousins and outspoken aunt—had not dared to ask. "People tend to draw romantic conclusions when they hear bits and pieces of events as told to them by some of the men I met in my travels. I assure you, I did not leave a trail of bloody bodies in my wake. I only did what was necessary to keep our government apprised of pertinent facts needed to plan strategies and judge the results of those strategies."

Mary shivered deliciously. "Imagine! One incident of incorrect reporting or incomplete information could have cost thousands of lives— maybe even lost the war. How modest you are, my lord, when it was you who single-handedly guided the direction of the entire war effort. No wonder my uncle speaks so highly of you. I vow I am impressed beyond measure!"

Tristan was taken aback by Mary's unaffected enthusiasm and high praise. He was also human enough to glory a bit in her display of esteem. Perhaps he had been overreacting—seeing guilt where there were only unanswered questions— after all, this wasn't the first time he had felt a niggle of doubt about his judgment of Mary Lawrence. She surely didn't sound like a Bonaparte sympathizer. She sounded very much like a devout patriot.

"Well," Mary was saying, with some heat, "I think it is absolutely criminal the way the War Office hasn't given you a single word of commendation, or even a cash settlement or title for all you have done. I wouldn't be in the least surprised if you weren't thoroughly disillusioned with us all—if you decided that Bonaparte was the better man after all."

She swiveled on the seat to look at him piercingly. "You aren't happy, are you, my lord, now that the war is at long last over? You must miss the excitement—I vow I would. With all that you know, it would be a simple matter for you to contact just the right people to effect Bonaparte's rescue from that pitiful island and transport him back to Paris. I'm sure the Emperor knows how to reward the people who serve him—unlike England, that bundles you off when it has no further use for you."

"You think my allegiance can be bought, Miss Lawrence?" Tristan asked dangerously, rising to the bait.

Ah, if only Jennie could be here to see her cousin finally getting his comeuppance! "Everyone has a price, my lord, whether it be in gold or by way of appealing to something deep inside that craves to be recognized," Mary nudged recklessly, glorying in her ability to finally get under this infuriating man's skin.

Rule's eyes narrowed as he stared at her. "And are you buying or selling, Miss Lawrence?"

CHAPTER FIVE

Mary knew she had gone too far. In her attempt to make him look guilty, and at the same time present herself as equally capable of treason, she had become overly ambitious—and stupidly careless.

She had meant to tease, to confuse, and to set him chasing madly after his own tail, but she hadn't planned on exposing her own neck to such an alarming degree. Lord, he looked fit to strangle her for the heartless traitor he took her to be—the scheming Bonapartist who dared suggest his loyalty could be bought.

She forced a silly giggle past her numb lips. "Whatever do you mean, my lord?" she asked, trying her utmost to look unintelligent—and only succeeding in appearing guilty as sin—"I was only funning. Far be it from me to suggest that—"

"That there are certain people who would like nothing better than to see Napoleon Bonaparte back on the throne in France, waging war against England again," Rule ended for her neatly, and with heavy sarcasm. "I don't find your assumptions amusing when they are applied to me, madam, and I can only question your reasons for broaching the subject at all."

You don't like it, do you? Mary shouted inwardly. Well, how do you think I feel each time you eye me like some butterfly on a pin? Aloud, she exclaimed, throwing up her hands in disgust, *"Sacrebleu!* You have caught me out, my lord. I confess! I'm a Bonapartist loyalist, sent to England to recruit volunteers to sail to Elba. Sir Henry was just an innocent pawn in my dastardly scheme; my reason for being here was to recruit you, England's grandest spy, over to our cause. I tried my utmost, but your loyalty to your mad king has proved too strong for my frail female wiles, which, heaven knows, I have used in excess in order to bring you to your knees at my feet. Alas, I must go to my fate, beaten but unbowed. *Vive la république!"* Her speech concluded, Mary folded her arms and awaited further developments, secretly wondering if association with this overzealous patriot had seriously unhinged her mind.

The silence that followed Mary's impassioned confession lasted until Rule had steered his curricle back out onto the street and relative privacy—and beyond. Once they had turned into the roadway fronting Sir Henry's residence, Rule commented, his voice sounding quite weary, "I have been playing the spy too long, Miss Lawrence, and have begun to see danger where none exists. Please accept my deepest apologies for ever having suspected you of any crime against England. It's obvious to me now that my aunt has told you of my conversation with her. I can understand now why you have gone out of your way to convince me of your guilt—waving so frantically at that poor hairdresser, for instance. It was meant to show just how ludicrous my assumptions were."

"Congratulations, my lord," Mary allowed, but not too graciously. "And here Rachel gave me the impression that you had to be hit on the head—

repeatedly—with a heavy red brick before you could be convinced of anything other than your own judgments. But I own myself astonished. Do you seriously mean you no longer view me as a member of a group plotting to free Bonaparte? You actually see me as innocent?"

Rule's spine straightened slightly. "You're no spy, Miss Lawrence, but you're not quite an innocent either. There's some mystery about you, I'd swear to that, but whatever it is, it's no business of mine—at least it won't be once I've convinced myself that you present no harm to Sir Henry or Rachel, or my cousins, who have befriended you for some reason."

"Like a dog with a bone, aren't you?" Mary sniffed, alighting from the curricle before Tristan could make a move to help her. "If I'm not a spy, I must be something else equally distasteful. Well, you know what, Lord High and Mighty Rule, you can just take your silly suspicions and your nasty little assumptions and—and *stuff them in your hat*!"

After emphatically nodding her head, as if to put a period to their discussion—and their relationship—Mary whirled away to ascend the steps to the house. But she turned at the top of the short flight to make one last statement—or threat: "And don't ever suppose I will stand up with you on the dance floor, for if you approach me I shall surely go into strong hysterics and kick you firmly in the shins!"

The heavy door slammed on the sight of her departing back as Tristan sat where he was, rubbing his chin in deep thought. She was a real termagant, this Miss Mary Lawrence, or whoever she really was.

Because of her, he found himself having to rethink his conclusions for the first time in a very long time—a prospect that cheered him far more than he expected. He wasn't exactly sure of just what the future held for the lady and himself, but one thing he knew for certain—she hadn't seen the last of him, not by a long chalk.

After all, there was still that tingle to consider . . . and now this strange *itch* . . . an itch that had begun to tantalize him as he watched Mary's trimly rounded bottom jiggling provocatively as she flounced away from him and up the steps.

It was the seventh heaven of the fashionable world, Almack's in the late spring of 1814, but to Tristan Rule it was a punishment worse than being forced by his fond mama at the tender age of twelve to stand up during a country dance with his cousin Lucy and be *oohed* and *aahed* at by a host of smiling relatives. Already he could see Lady Jersey measuring him from between narrowed eyelids, wondering whether or not she could coerce, bully, or otherwise persuade him into partnering any of the limp wallflowers that seemed to consider Almack's their own private hothouse.

But there was nothing else for it—as it was Wednesday, and if he were to seek *her* out this evening, Almack's was the logical place to start. Not that he planned to single her out for anything as ridiculous as the Scottish reel now in progress, even if the celebrated violinist, Niel Gow, was the one sawing away on the strings. He winced involuntarily as Lord Worcester whirled by with Lady Harriett Butler, the two of them panting and sweating like dray horses after a long run.

The things I won't do for my country, Tristan thought to himself as he pushed his lean body away from the pillar he had been reclining against and began another seemingly leisurely stroll around the rooms, his dark eyes searching—ever searching—for a sight of Mary Lawrence.

It was nearing the hour of eleven when at last his vigilance was rewarded and he espied his Aunt Rachel entering the vestibule, her tardy charge in tow. Mary was in looks tonight as, he reminded himself with a snicker of self-derision, she was every night, drat the infuriating chit anyhow. After disposing of her shimmering taffeta cloak, now being lovingly carried away by one of the stewards, Mary turned to face the ballroom and gave the assembled guests their first glimpse of her ivory-colored gown (that complemented her gleaming ivory shoulders and half-exposed bosom perfectly, Tristan could not help but notice). The entire bodice of the gown, along with at least ten inches of the hem and demi-train, were lavishly sprinkled with diamante dewdrops that winked and glistened with every move she made, every breath she took.

Twinkling diamonds lent an extra sparkle to her dark curls and glittered in her ears—even her dainty slippers were adorned with brilliant diamante bows. On another woman the abundance of sparkle would have appeared overdone, even slightly vulgar, but Mary carried it off beautifully. All around him Tristan heard the indrawn breaths of jealous debutantes and the hissing whispers of their disgruntled mamas, while the comments of the gentlemen within earshot only served to start a fire in Lord Rule's blood that had little to do with his zealous interest in the welfare of his homeland.

He was drawn to Mary's side almost without realizing he had moved, and the dozen or so hopeful swains who harbored plans of their own concerning Miss Lawrence hastily stepped off in other directions, unwilling to challenge Ruthless

Rule's claim to the Incomparable for the country dance just forming.

The sparkle of Mary's attire dimmed beside the hard glitter now in her huge green eyes. After the way they had parted only that afternoon—and most especially after she had issued her threat to physically assault him if he ever dared approach her again—she had wondered about this meeting, even fantasized about it a bit, picturing the arrogant Lord Rule hopping about some ballroom in his elegant black dress, looking for all the world like a huge crow flapping its wings as he favored his injured shin.

But now reality, in the form of that infuriating man himself, was staring her straight in the eye, daring her to make cakes out of both of them within the most hallowed, and most prestigious, walls of Almack's. Almack's—the holy grail of young English womanhood, ever longed for, prayed over, dreamed about, and once attained, cherished close to her bosom forevermore. Damn his devious soul! she cried inwardly—he knows I can't make a scene here. He knows it and is standing there smirking at me, laughing at me, because once again he has won and I have lost.

But then Mary remembered her plans for this evening, plans she had somehow been reluctant to cancel even after Rule's admission that afternoon that he no longer considered her to be a French spy. Why not? she thought as she swallowed down hard on her pride and smiled at her worst enemy, holding out one French kid-encased hand to accept his invitation to join the other young couples on the floor.

As Tristan smiled at her knowingly, being human enough to savor the moment of his triumph—and male enough to be so foolish as to show it—Mary's gloved fingertips bit hurtingly into his forearm, reminding him once more that this particular kitten, although she looked so outwardly soft and cuddly, was not averse to using her claws. He may have satisfied himself that she was not the person he had been told to seek—the English connection in a Continent-wide plot to free Napoleon—but she was still an unanswered question in his mind. And Tristan didn't like unanswered questions. For all he knew, she could be twice as dangerous as the conspirator he sought, both to his friend and mentor Sir Henry and his cousins Lucy and Jennie.

Yes, he told himself as they parted momentarily due to the movements of the dance, he mustn't allow Miss Lawrence's obvious beauty and charm to blind him to the very real fact that now he had not one, but *two* problems. He held out his hand to Mary, leading her into the next movement of the dance even as he assessed her yet again, looking for clues he was not certain he would recognize even if they were pushed into his face, and wished once more for the simplicity of war, where your enemies were so much easier to spot. "You are, as usual, in fine looks this evening, Miss Lawrence," he baited her as they rubbed shoulders lightly before moving on, "and that heightened color in your cheeks is most flattering."

I believe I just might murder that man, Mary mused satisfyingly as she whirled out of earshot for a moment. "I do confess to feeling a bit of excitement, sir," she owned sweetly as they faced each other yet again. "I had heard so much about Almack's, you know, but the reality far exceeds the dream. Did you ever see so many exalted personages in one place at one time? I vow I am impressed!"

"You impress easily, Miss Lawrence," Tristan

responded, taking her elbow as the dance drew to its conclusion and guiding her to a pair of chairs at the side of the room.

Mary looked up at him, her head tilted prettily to one side. "Oh, I doubt that, my lord, else I would be in a constant swoon at being so openly pursued by the famous Lord Rule. As it is, I cannot be more unmoved by the prospect. Do you think I am unnatural, my lord?"

Tristan sat himself down beside her, looking off into the distance as he did, and sending shivers down the spine of no less than seven gentlemen who had rashly decided to ask Miss Lawrence for the next dance. "We have already established the fact that you don't like me above half, Miss Lawrence. Do you really find it necessary to belabor the point?"

"I do, since you refuse to take the hint and *go away*!" Mary was pushed to exclaim before carefully busying herself playing with the silken tassel at the end of her fan. "Aunt Rachel said you always were a bit *thick*, but even an absolute dolt would have cut rope by now. What do you want from me, what assurance of innocence will it take, before you realize that you are wasting your time dreaming up intrigues in which I play a part?"

Turning his dark head slowly in her direction, Tristan said in a low, steely voice: "Tell me your name."

The previously folded fan unfurled and began beating the air in front of Mary's flushed face. "You are being absurd, sir, yet again," she pointed out with what she hoped was amusement. "You know my name."

"I know the name you go by, the one Sir Henry chose for you when first he established you in Sussex ten years ago, but I seriously doubt that Mary Lawrence—that simple, unassuming appelation—comes within a dozen miles of being the one that appears on some parish records somewhere."

The fan was beginning to stir up a mighty breeze. "My, haven't you been the busy one," Mary remarked, all humor gone from her voice. "Hot-footed it down to Sussex, did you, to see what dirt you could dig up at my expense? And what else, pray tell, did you find?"

Tristan leaned back on the uncomfortable chair and recited informatively: "You were an apt pupil in penmanship and the use of maps, although you persisted in drawing Italy to look more like a riding boot than your governess thought permissible. You despised needlework although your sampler was more than passable in my opinion. As a horsewoman you have few equals, even if you earned the undying animosity of several of the local gentry by running your horse across the trail of the fox in a deliberate attempt to save the poor hunted creature."

Mary smiled a bit at the remembrance of that little bit of foolishness, but then her indignation returned. "And that is all, my lord? Surely you have left out the time I poured honey down Miss Penelope Blakestone's bodice at a picnic because she was making sheep's eyes at young Jeremy Stone when she knew full well that I was deep in love with him myself."

"You were thirteen at the time, so I disregarded it," Tristan put in smoothly, making Mary wish she had a handy pitcher of honey hidden in her reticule at that very moment.

Closing the fan with a definite snap, Mary rose to her feet, causing Tristan to scramble a bit as he strove to unwind his long legs and follow suit. "You are a rude, snooping, mischief-making *monster*!" Mary cried, clearly unable to carry on any pretense that she cared not a snap for his ridiculous investigation of her past. "How *dare* you pry into my life that way! What earthly reason could you have given all those people when you went about snooping into something that was never your concern? How can I ever show my face in Sussex again after what you have done?"

"Do you want to?" Rule asked tauntingly.

Mary's eyes narrowed dangerously as she looked up into his unrevealing face. "No, damn you, I don't want to! But that's beside the point. I should tell Sir Henry what you are about, that's what I should do, and then we would see just who would be laughing, you cad."

Tristan took her elbow in a firm grip and began guiding her over to his Aunt Rachel, who was sitting with the dowagers and looking utterly bored with the whole spectacle of Almack's. "You'll tell Sir Henry nothing, Miss Lawrence— you haven't done so yet, or else I should have been called into his office for a thorough dressing down long since. It would seem he sees you as purity itself, and protects you like you were his own."

"Well, then? If Sir Henry, who, you'll have to agree, knows everything about me, is not concerned or fearful of allowing me in polite society, why can't you just accept me as I am?"

"Sir Henry's judgment may be clouded by something or someone out of the past. I am objective. Even if you are innocent of any wrongdoing, your mere existence may give someone power over Sir Henry, power that could even force that patriotic man into actions detrimental to England. The mere fact that your 'uncle' refuses to confide in me makes me suspect something very deep and dangerous." Tristan drew Mary to a halt and turned her to him one more time. "Now are you willing to tell me your name. For Sir Henry's sake?"

"Mary, Queen of Scots!" Mary Lawrence snapped before jerking her elbow loose and completing her journey over to Rachel on her own.

It was very late, and the dance floor was crowded with couples eager to wedge one more dance into the evening, when Mary, still observed by Lord Rule, walked unescorted onto one of the wide balconies outside the main room.

The small raggedly dressed man who crept steathily out of the shadows approached the girl on quiet feet and the two exchanged a few furiously whispered words before a much-folded paper changed hands, and the man, the paper now stuffed inside his shabby coat, slid back into the shadows.

Mary was just placing one slippered foot back into the main room when Tristan Rule vaulted nimbly over the balcony railing to land on the balls of his feet in the soft underbrush that edged the small garden. Hanging back discreetly out of sight, Rule watched as the small man reappeared under a dim gas lamp, then made off down the street in the direction of Piccadilly. Waiting until he could mentally reach the count of ten, Rule then started after the man, intent on following wherever he led.

While Lord Rule, using talents he developed during long years in His Majesty's service, ducked into doorways and hid behind drainpipes as he followed the small man deep into the bowels of Jack Ketch's warren, Mary Lawrence was taking her leave of Almack's Assembly Rooms, first taking care to thank Jennie Wilde for the loan of her man Ben for the evening.

CHAPTER SIX

Mary was sitting alone in the breakfast room the next morning, still savoring her first victory over Ruthless Rule. Jennie had sent around a note earlier, describing Ben's elation at having eluded his pursuer after leading him a merry dance until the wee hours of the morning.

This single success had naturally led the volatile Mary into considering other relatively harmless pranks aimed at keeping Lord Rule out of sight while she tried to make the best of what was left of the Season. Already she realized one flaw in last night's plan: she should have had Ben appear much earlier in the evening, then she could have avoided their confrontation on the dance floor altogether. Ah well, as a fledgling conspirator, she couldn't believe she had done that poorly overall.

Now that she knew exactly why Tristan was dogging her—believing her very existence to be a danger to Sir Henry and the national security— she knew she could proceed without fear of her adopted uncle's censure if he should ever discover what she was about. After all, if Sir Henry had wanted Tristan to know her history, he would have told him long since. Besides, she assured herself as she buttered a second muffin, it wasn't as if she were really a danger to Sir Henry—being French was no longer considered a sin in London.

Actually, she couldn't understand Sir Henry's insistence that she hide her heritage from the world.

The matter of the plot to rescue Napoleon from Elba, the plot Tristan had told her was his reason for suspecting her in the first place, was really none of her concern. Wiser heads than hers, notably Sir Henry's, would certainly scotch any such attempts before they could be born. Napoleon was defeated, soundly and forever. After all, wasn't all London gearing up for a gigantic round of celebrations even now? Surely all London couldn't be wrong—no matter what that ridiculous Lord Rule said to the contrary.

Having eased her conscience all around, Mary was just about to rise from the table and go in search of Rachel, who had been closeted in her rooms tussling over a minor snag in the tale of her hero and heroine, just then at each other's throats over a silly misunderstanding that was throwing up boulders in the path of True Love, when she was surprised to see Dexter Rutherford enter the room, a sheepish expression on his face.

"Dexter," Mary greeted him, "I see the operation was a success. You have actually succeeded in separating yourself from Lord Rule. My congratulations to your physician, and may I please have his directions as I too am in need of his services."

Dexter stopped dead in his tracks, examining his person as if looking for signs of recent surgery, before coloring brightly and chuckling weakly. "Oh, you're funning me, aren't you? I admit to admiring Tristan—he's a capital fellow, you know—but it ain't as if I'm living in his pocket."

"That's a relief, seeing as how the man seems to be trying to live in *mine*. Having you in there too just might make me list more than a little to one side, don't you think?" Mary teased the young man before waving him into a chair. "To what do I owe the honor of this visit, or am I mistaken and it is Aunt Rachel you have come to see?"

Dexter ran a nervous finger around his suddenly too-tight cravat (a glorious creation that flattered his valet no end). "*Ac-tu-ally*," he squeaked, "it was the two of you. It seems I find myself in need of some reputable females to act as companions for a young lady I'm seeing."

Mary shook her head. "Not that I'm doubting that you have a problem, Dex, but what about Lucy or Jennie? Surely they're reputable."

The young man became fairly agitated, twisting in his chair as if he had just discovered a nettle in his breeches. "Those two—good God, as if I need those busybodies poking into my life, matchmaking, and twitting me unmercifully! No, I'm not that stupid that I'd lay my head on that block! I thought about getting m'friend Bertie Sandover's sister to help, but she's known me forever and threatened to tell Kitty everything about me—can't have that, can I?"

"Kitty?" Mary prompted, barely suppressing a giggle at the thought of the turmoil Jennie and Lucy could cause once they scented a romance in the air. Poor Dexter, he'd have to be truly desperate to let either of those ladies in on his plans.

Now Dexter's complexion turned a deep, fiery red. "Kitty Toland," he gushed, lowering his head. "She's only seventeen and the most beautiful woman in England—in the entire world! Her brother, Jerome Toland, is not averse to my suit, you understand, but he says Kitty must only see me if she is accompanied by trustworthy companions. I thought and thought, and at last I came up with you and Rachel."

"Any port in a storm, eh, Dexter?" Mary could not help but tease, enjoying herself more than a little bit at the young man's expense.

Dexter's expression became pained as he realized he had really put his foot in it—again. Why was it that he had inherited none of the suave, debonair talents of his cousin Julian? "I know I'm saying this badly—it's a habit of mine, you know—but you know what it is, it's that I think I'm in love. Never thought it would happen—kind of damps you, actually, but there it is, and I confess I'm not really sure how to do anything anymore."

Mary rose and walked around the table to place a commiserating arm around the young man's shoulders. "Ah, poor Dexter. What a beast I am for teasing you when you're so obviously in torment. Of course Rachel and I will help you however we can. Why don't we adjourn to the morning room and you can tell me all about your Kitty Toland. Such a pretty name, Kitty."

"*Ac-tu-ally*, it's Catherine." Dexter informed her as they walked arm in arm down the corridor to the morning room. Once there he proceeded to tell her more—definitely more than Mary decided she *ac-tu-ally* cared to know—about this paragon of a female who had snared his bachelor heart.

Beside her youth, Kitty was the very worst sort of female for Dexter to have come across, for she was also a Total Innocent. The young Lothario was well and truly smitten, and had been from the moment his roving eye first encountered the shy, blond beauty from Cornwall.

"She doesn't know *anything*, Mary, nothing at all. It's like setting a baby loose in a stable full of stallions to see her surrounded by all the dandies and rakes who'd like nothing more than to ruin her. She has little fortune, you understand, and for some reason that seems to make her fair game for all the randy—er—well, never mind," he ended hurriedly.

"That's all right, Dex, I believe I understand," Mary said, easing his discomfiture. "Rachel, hinting broadly of my *vast* dowry—compliments of Sir Henry—scotched any such ideas by some of the more pressing of my admirers early in the Season. Now I am only beset by penniless fortune hunters, but then no one can have every little wrinkle smoothed out for them, can they?"

"Jerome is trying so very hard, too," Dexter pressed on, clearly thinking in one track and not even bothering to comment on Mary's problem. "He's her guardian, you know, the parents having died of some disease caught from putrid drains, or something. They're shockingly to let, which is why Jerome's run of luck at one of the private gaming hells was so fortuitous. Instead of then gambling or wenching—sorry, Mary—it all away, he hied himself straight to Cornwall to bring Kitty to town and launch her so that she could find herself a proper husband." He turned to look at Mary intently. "It would be a bleeding waste to give her to some bumpkin farmer, really it would. She's a jewel—a diamond of the first water—truly she is. I can only marvel that she likes me even a little bit."

"I must meet this paragon," Mary mused, almost to herself.

"Oh! How happy I am that you say so," Dexter fairly shouted, hopping to his feet. "I'll bring her round this afternoon so that the three of you can get acquainted. You'll love her," he promised, already sprinting toward the hallway, "you'll absolutely *adore* her!"

Mary laid her head against the back of the chair, smiling broadly. *"Absolutely,* you lovesick looby." She chuckled happily before rising to seek out

Rachel and tell her of their expected visitor. "After all, why should Jennie and Lucy have all the fun?"

While Mary and Rachel were giggling like schoolgirls over the thought of a smitten Dexter waxing poetic over a beautiful child from the wilds of Cornwall, Tristan Rule was just rising from the bed he had lain in only a few, frustrating hours. What a profitless evening his had been—chasing through the slimy gutters and over the sooty rooftops of the worst section of London in pursuit of some crafty jackanapes who had had the temerity to elude him in the end.

Had Mary been passing instructions to the man —or had the man been collecting payment in exchange for his silence? Was Mary a conspirator, or the victim of blackmail? Oh, his head ached from all the questions that were rattling around inside, none of them with easy answers. If only Sir Henry were willing to take him into his confidence. Already he had wasted precious time believing Mary to be a French spy, giving the true conspirator free rein to continue with his plans.

Now that he knew she was not involved with the plan to free Napoleon, Rule felt real relief, but discovering that Mary Lawrence didn't exist until ten years ago had opened up an entirely new, different, kettle of fish that didn't smell that much better than the last one. There was something particularly distasteful, even dangerous, about Mary's past, something so volatile that Sir Henry, who had never hidden anything from Tristan before, was insisting on playing all his cards very close to his chest.

If someone besides Tristan, someone with either blackmail or treason on his mind, discovered even the little bit that Tristan had unearthed on his quick journey into Sussex, there was no end to the amount of trouble Mary Lawrence's presence in Sir Henry's house could mean for England.

Throwing back the tangled covers, Rule leaped to his feet and stomped over to the washstand to pour a pitcher of cold water over his tousled black locks. Rising from this punishment sputtering and shivering, shaking his head like a dog coming out of an icy stream, he rang for his man and then grabbed up his robe, tying the silken sash around his waist with a vengeance. "Damn that green-eyed minx for not trusting me!" he swore to the room at large, flinging himself into a chair, his black stare serving to unnerve his valet more than a little bit as that man entered the room, a steaming cup of coffee balanced before him on a silver tray.

"Women!" Tristan sputtered, eyeing his man as if daring him to say something, anything, in that gender's defense.

"Indeed, m'lord." The servant gulped, already backing toward the door. "An' sure Oi am that we'd all be the better fer it if we could but live widout 'em."

"*I can,*" Tristan gritted before taking a large gulp of the too-hot coffee. "Damn it all anyway—I *will!*"

CHAPTER SEVEN

On the thirtieth of May the first Peace of Paris was signed in that city, giving yet another excuse to the celebration-mad populace of London to don their finery and make absolute cakes of themselves by eating, dancing, and imbibing to the top of their bent and beyond.

One of the more sedate parties, a modest Venetian breakfast for no more than six hundred of the host and hostess's closest and dearest friends, was held near Richmond Park. That this breakfast did not commence until three in the afternoon, and was not expected to wind to a close much before the wee hours of the morning, meant little. The mood of the invited guests was jovial, even jubilant, the seemingly endless supply of strong drink notwithstanding.

Mary was in attendance, accompanied by Miss Kitty Toland, whom she and Rachel had agreed to chaperon, a circumstance that meant that Dexter Rutherford was also a member of their party. Indeed, as Mary had whispered to Rachel a few moments earlier in the carriage, it would have taken one of Congreve's rocket's being strapped to his hindquarters and the fuse lit to blast Dexter away from his ladylove.

But then it was nice to have a gentleman in their party, since it was he who took charge of matters such as securing a comfortable, shady spot under a tree and then chasing after servants to secure some nourishment before they all wilted from hunger. Not that Mary would have had too much trouble convincing one of her flirts to play fetch and carry for her, but it had become so fatiguing to have to explain her association with the dangerous Tristan Rule to her apprehensive swains that she was just as glad not to have to go to the bother.

She had hoped that Rule's absence from her side for the past four days had scotched all those rumors she knew to be flying fast and furious about the *ton*, but she hadn't counted on the lack of starch her beaux had evinced when faced with the prospect of being thought to be poaching on Ruthless Rule's preserves. "It's like I have a sign hanging from my back that says 'Private Property —Trespassers Beware,' " Mary had complained to Rachel more times than that weary woman wished to remember, "and I don't know who angers me most—that dratted man or the silly fools who act as if he were some sort of furious Greek god who just might start hurling lightning bolts at them or something if they dare to cross him."

Even more infuriating, at least to Mary's mind, was the fact that she actually had found herself *looking* for the pesky man, and wondering just where he was that he had left off spending his time making her life as miserable as possible. Sir Henry had mentioned something or other that hinted of Rule being out and about the King's business, but no amount of prompting could nudge the older man into saying a thing more. "Probably out minding mice at crosswalks or some such important task," Mary had said, sniffing inelegantly, causing her guardian no end of amusement.

Whatever the reason for his absence, Mary was left to punish herself with the knowledge that it had left a large hole in her life—one that she would have sworn she craved more than a personal invitation to Carleton House to meet the Czar's sister, the Grand Duchess Catherine of Oldenburg. In fact, she thought, blushing yet again as she reclined in a studied pose beneath a leafy tree, she had been thinking altogether too much about Tristan Rule—about his dark good looks, his intense black eyes, the barely leashed power hidden beneath the stark black he chose to wear, his lips, cool and firm against hers for the length of a kiss stolen in the moonlight.

And that was the worst—that she couldn't help remembering that kiss, that deliberate insult that had seemed to amuse him as much as it still haunted her. How could she be attracted to a man who thought she was capable of destroying Sir Henry—indeed, all of England, if she truly believed his ridiculous claims! What perverse imp of nature had so constructed a woman that she could thoroughly loathe a man and at the same time search her horizons constantly just for the sight of his disdainful, condemning face?

Mary shook her head dismissingly and determinedly set out to change the flow of her thoughts, choosing to observe Kitty Toland and Dexter Rutherford as they sat yards apart on the blanket a servant had spread and stared at each other with blissfully vacant eyes. Try as she could, Mary could not see the attraction, either Kitty's for Dexter or his for her.

Not that Kitty wasn't a pretty girl, for she was; all pink and blond and still carrying a bit of nursery plumpness, with china-blue eyes that had a tendency to stare unwaveringly at nothing in particular in a way Mary couldn't force herself to believe reflected any great intelligence. Besides, the girl had a lamentable habit of saying, "*Oh, Gemini!*" before nearly every sentence she uttered, until Rachel had run posthaste to her rooms, inspiration for yet another character for her novel taking the form of a hair-witted debutante who spoke only in exclamations.

Dexter, for his part, wasn't exactly the sort from which storybook heroes were made. He was neither bold, nor dashing, and his conversation certainly couldn't rival anything written by the Bard, but when it came to portraying the sillier side of being struck with one of Cupid's tiny darts, Dex bore off the palm. Soulful sighs, yearning looks, and garbled speech may not have been designed to set Mary's heart to pitter-pattering, but they seem to have turned the trick for Dexter when it came to winning the adoration of his Kitty. It was, Mary had informed Rachel the previous evening after the two of them had spent long, trying hours watching the two lovebirds coo at each other unintelligibly, as if some kind spirit had seen two halves of the same whole and quickly arranged for the two adorable nincompoops to find each other and become one great, amorous ninny, sure to populate the next generation with yet another set of incompetents in search of mates.

"Want an apple, Miss Toland?" Dex asked just then, if only to prove Mary's point.

"Oh, Gemini, I would like one above all things," Kitty simpered, her blushing cheeks looking like fine, ripe apples themselves. "But, oh, Gemini, how ever could I, when it is wearing that awful peel?"

Puffing out his thin chest just as if he had been asked to slay yon dragon to prove his love, Dex then fairly scrambled toward the large picnic

hamper before the hovering servant could
efficiently pare away the peel on a shiny apple he
had already snatched up in preparation of being
asked to perform just such a service, and wrestled
both knife and apple from the poor young fellow.
"It would be a pleasure, an *honor*, to remove this
offensive covering so that you should not injure
those fair lips and those delicate white teeth,"
Dexter vowed fervently as Mary and the dumb-
struck servant desperately tried to look anywhere
but at the young swain as he proceeded to
mutilate the innocent fruit, putting his left thumb
in imminent danger of being peeled as well.

"No accounting for tastes, is there?" Rachel offered, having approached the scene while Mary
was otherwise occupied and was just then sitting
herself down on the chair another servant had
secured for her. "I had to discard my idea of
patterning a character after the girl, though. After
I had her say hello, I found she had precious little
additional to add to the conversation. I didn't
realize how difficult it is to find inconsequential
things to say—do you think that means I'm a blue-
stocking? Perhaps that's why I've been left so
firmly on the shelf all these years."

"You're bright blue through and through,
Aunt," Mary confirmed, then added, "but your
mind is not what has kept you from the altar. It's
your foolish pride that keeps you and Sir Henry
from making a match of things. Isn't it time you
forgave him for a young man's indiscretion?"

Rachel looked at her charge, her confusion easy
to read in her face. "Henry's indiscretion? Whatever are you jabbering about? It wasn't Henry
who destroyed our engagement. It was *my*
indis—" Rachel's voice broke off suddenly as she
realized what she had been about to say.

Perhaps the sun was too warm on her head,

Mary thought as she reached to retrieve the bonnet she had discarded earlier. How could she have been so mistaken? From the few slips Sir Henry had made in her presence, she felt sure that he was the one responsible for the termination of the engagement just a week before the wedding. But now Rachel was saying Sir Henry was the injured party and she the one who had done something to cause the breach. "Forgive me for being so presumptuous, especially with a woman who is supposed to be my mentor of sorts," Mary apologized with a singular lack of contriteness, "but I do believe the time has come for you and my so-intelligent uncle to sit down together and go over the particulars of your estrangement in a bit more detail. Somebody seems to have scrambled the facts a bit, if I'm right."

"I don't care for a sad rehashing of long-ago sins, Mary," Rachel replied almost regally. "I have done my penance by donning my caps and playing the loving aunt to a series of nieces and nephews as they found their way into the world and beyond the need of my care. Why, seeing Lucy safely raised and launched was more than enough atonement for a dozen sins worse than my fleeting infatuation with Lord Hether—er—Mary! Isn't that Tristan over there, beside the buffet table?"

Rachel's impulsive confession was enough to keep Mary's attention riveted to her even if Mother Nature had at that moment decided to shower the assembled guests with hail the size of oranges, but nothing could keep her attentive once Tristan's name was mentioned. "Where?" she asked, already craning her neck in the direction Rachel had named. "Oh, drat, there he is, looking booted and spurred and ready to ride, as usual." Realizing she was looking more than a little interested in the man, she quickly busied herself retying her bonnet strings, asking Rachel in a whisper, "Is he looking this way? Does he see me? Don't wave to him, maybe he'll go away. How do I look? Drat this hot sun, I vow I look as wilted as yesterday's flowers."

Rachel could barely hide her smile as she watched Mary lost in uncharacteristic confusion, and silently congratulated herself at settling both her current charge and her troublesome nephew with so little fuss. Oh, Lucy and Jennie would doubtless take all the credit for the match, but that didn't bother Rachel. She only wished to have everyone neatly established so that she could leave London as soon as possible. Her plan to live quietly in the city had been foolish, she saw now, but who could have foreseen Henry coming to beg a favor of her after the way she had disgraced him all those years ago? She hadn't written a word of her novel since going to live in Henry's house— was only using the novel as the camouflage she would need once Mary was safely married and her past buried once and for all beneath her new husband's name—but Henry wasn't to know that. Just as he wasn't to know that she still loved him with every fiber of her being—for as much good that would do her when she was scribbling away in some cottage at the back of beyond.

What Rachel knew she definitely didn't need was to have Mary sticking her inquisitive little nose into affairs that were none of her business. If she had kept her past indiscretions a secret from Lucy and Jennie—and especially from Tristan— all these years, she was not about to allow Mary to stir up all that old heartache now! Thank heavens for Tristan, Rachel rejoiced silently, marveling as she did so that she would ever have reason to thank Tristan for anything, for he would keep Mary too busy for any dangerous snooping. So thinking, Rachel decided to give the struggling romance a bit of a nudge. "Does he see us, you ask?" she answered Mary just as that young woman was about to take another covert peek herself. "Why, yes, if that marvelous smile is any indication, I do believe he has. My goodness, do I mistake my man? I almost believe Tristan to actually have a certain *spring* to his step as he makes his way to us."

"He's probably just come from turning two hapless souls over to the high executioner for speaking French in a public place. Just the sort of thing to cheer him up, I do believe," Mary snapped, but her words held no real sting.

"Oh, Mary, you mustn't refine too long on Tristan's little follies," Rachel interposed, trying to calm the waters before this meeting between the two ended in yet another useless confrontation. "He has apologized for believing you part of that French plot—besides, Henry told me just this morning that they have captured three men who supposedly were working to raise funds for a ship to sail to Elba. Why, that may explain Tristan's absence these last days, don't you think?" But before Mary, whose head had come up with a jerk at Rachel's words, could answer, the older woman gave a very uncharacteristic shriek. "Oh, Lord, Tristan! *No!*"

Mary looked first to her companion and then, with some shock, toward the buffet table, where she had last seen Tristan, looking so dangerously handsome. But he wasn't there. He was running full tilt to place himself in front of the runaway curricle being dragged along behind a pair of wild-eyed stallions before it could cut a path of death and destruction through the throng of assembled guests.

Tristan had ridden hard most of the night in

order to get back to London, the three conspirators he had run to ground in a hedgerow tavern near Maidstone having been handed over to the trustworthy agents Sir Henry had so fortuitously supplied.

His haste was hard to explain, even to himself, considering his oft-spoken distaste for silly affairs like this Venetian breakfast, but he knew Mary was to be in attendance and that thought served as the spur that had sent him galloping along the moonlit paths that led to the city. It was juvenile really, this burning desire to report the success of his mission to Mary in person, but he could not help but harbor the hope that the arrest he had made would put him back in Mary's good graces—if indeed he was ever there in the first place. At least she would be made to see that he had not entirely been hunting out mare's nests when he was investigating her background. After all, there *had* been a plot to free Napoleon, and the arrests proved it.

Of course, there was still that little matter of her true identity—and Rule's fear that she presented a danger to Sir Henry if there was even a trace of scandal in her past. Tristan wasn't about to turn a blind eye to that possibility, no matter how uncomfortable he felt about his earlier, erroneous assumption that Mary Lawrence could be in the pay of some French conspirators.

No, he remained adamant in his determination to uncover whatever secret Mary and Sir Henry were so steadfastly protecting, but he had used his hours on horseback the previous night to rethink his tactics. He would pretend he had given up the investigation and concentrate on courting Mary, winning his way into her good graces. He would do this to protect national security, he had told himself then, just as he tried to tell himself again at that moment—that electrifying moment when he had looked across the expanse of green lawn and felt his heart do a strange little leap in his chest as he caught sight of her sitting beneath the shade of an old tree, looking the picture of beauty, youth, and innocence.

All his weariness had disappeared in an instant, and he had felt his usually expressionless features soften involuntarily into a wide, unaffected smile as his feet had immediately began propelling him along the straightest path to her side. He couldn't wait to tell Mary about his exploits of the previous evening—just like a small boy proudly showing off his first racing cup to his parents.

He had taken no more than a half dozen steps, and was just raising a hand to wave to his aunt, when he sensed rather than saw that something was wrong. Swinging to his right, he espied the driverless curricle careening down the lengthy incline, two heaving, foam-flecked horses galloping ahead of it in the shafts.

The peaceful scene was shattered within an instant. Where moments ago happy groups had either been strolling arm in arm over the closely clipped lawns or reclining at their ease at the base of shade-giving trees, there was now the sharp, sickening smell of panic—the sight of fashionably clad ladies and top-o'-the-trees gentlemen scurrying like colorful ants to and fro searching for cover, the sound of high-pitched screams and baritone curses.

But Tristan saw none of this, heard none of this. Immediately his senses were concentrated on the horses and the curricle that bounced behind it in imminent danger of overturning. His muscles tautened, preparing for action, and his heart began to beat more rapidly, sending his heated blood pulsing through his veins as he quickly calculated his options, weighed his alternatives.

Darting a quick glance behind him, he saw that the fleeing guests had somehow created an area of open ground that led straight to the small, ornamental pond that lay at almost a right angle to the course the horses were taking. His dark eyes narrowing, Tristan's agile brain rapidly mapped a possible course of action and he whirled to set off at a dead run, planning to intercept the rampaging horses before they could get past him.

He ran swiftly, surely, to the spot he had chosen, sparing only a second to glance in Mary's direction, silently praying that she and his aunt had had the good sense to position themselves behind a tree. They had—a white-faced Rachel holding on fiercely to Mary, who seemed to be struggling to be free, while Dexter stood staunchly in front of some blond creature who was just then sobbing into his coat sleeve.

Then the thunder of galloping hooves and the loud clatter of the rapidly disintegrating curricle commanded his full attention, and Tristan spread his legs slightly for balance, flexed his knees, and extended his arms in front of him, his hands open, his fingers tensed, waiting . . . waiting . . .

He could smell the hot breath of the horse nearest him, see clearly the white of one of its rolling eyes, feel the sharp flick of its mane against his hands.

Now! his brain screamed. *Now!*

Mary broke free of Rachel's clinging hands and was just about to run toward Tristan when he reached out with both his strong, tanned hands— with those long, lean fingers she had told herself fitted his reputation for ruthlessness so perfectly —and grabbed two handfuls of mane, while at the same time leaping into the air, to end up landing himself neatly astride the horse's back.

"He's going to try for the leads!" Mary screamed to Rachel, who had hidden her head in her hands. "Oh, Tristan, be careful!"

Mary saw Tristan's head lying flush against the horse's neck as he reached across the space separating the two horses and made a grab for the other's halter. Then the curricle was past her, still traveling at a furious pace, but now being directed by Ruthless Rule, who had somehow gained control of the leads.

The horses changed direction, heading toward the pond that sat about two hundred yards away on the left. Mary ran along behind, her skirts lifted immodestly as she willingly sacrificed propriety for speed. It wasn't over yet, she knew, although she silently agreed with Rule that running the horses into the pond was the best chance he had of stopping them before any more damage was done.

Please let him be all right, the reckless fool! she begged any deities that may have been listening, then shook her head at the ridiculousness of her thoughts. Ruthless Rule—Reckless Fool—they even rhymed! Oh, whatever possessed the man, to have him taking such unthinking chances with his life? And what sort of brainless ninny am I to have even entertained the thought of going to his rescue before his masculine tendency to act the hero got him trampled into the dust? Anyone would think I'd cared one way or the other about the man!

Not that these unpleasant thoughts slowed Mary's pace—she continued to race full tilt toward the pond, where she had seen a large splash just scant seconds earlier. By the time she reached the banks of the water the runaway horses were standing with their heads down in the shafts, their flanks still shuddering as they seemed to be trying to understand just what had happened to them.

Where was Rule? The curricle, which had once

been a glorious equipage painted in scarlet with gold trim, lay on its side, half submerged in the pond, and Mary's fearful heart skipped a beat as she pictured Tristan pinned beneath the surface by one of the curricle's wheels.

She was just about to plunge her own body into the water when the surface of the pond was broken by Tristan's dark head and broad shoulders, as he rose to his feet to stand more than waist deep in the water, his attention fixed on releasing the exhausted horses from the shafts.

"Did you see that?" Dexter Rutherford fairly shouted in Mary's ear as he came up beside her, his awestruck gaze stuck fast to the sight of his hero. "What a first-rate sight that was! Puts those devil-dares at Astley's Circus to the blush, that's what it does. Isn't Tris a prime one, Miss Lawrence? Oh, I wouldn't have missed this for the world!"

By now Mary and Dexter were only a small part of a much larger audience. From all sides came the multitude of guests and scores of servants, all chattering, applauding, and generally acting as if Tristan Rule had single-handedly saved their lives —which he may very well have done. Several young bucks were sufficiently enthused as to plunge Hessians-first into the water, bent on helping the man of the hour lead the team of horses back to shore.

Mary watched Rule closely as his long strides cut waves through the water, bringing him closer to her with every step. His black hair was pasted to his head, showing off his handsome, chiseled features almost as advantageously as his clinging wet coat and pantaloons did his fine physique. Indeed, among the cheers and shouts of congratulations Mary heard more than one feminine gasp and giggle of appreciation.

For reasons Mary did not choose to investigate,

this unconscious flaunting of his physical person served to touch off a spark of anger deep inside her that temporarily banished her earlier concern for his safety.

As Tristan mounted the bank to stand not three feet away from her, she tilted her determined chin toward the afternoon sun and remarked sarcastically, "Ah, if it isn't the knight errant. Good thing you left your suit of armor at home, sir, else you'd be rusted into a statue before you could enjoy all the hosannas of your many admirers."

What the deuce was the matter with the girl now? Tristan asked himself in righteous confusion. Anyone would think I stopped the curricle just to upset her. And to think I rode half the night just to open myself to more of her insults!

Bowing deeply from the waist, a move that caused one dark, wet lock of hair to fall into a roguishly becoming curl on his forehead, Tristan replied coolly, "On the contrary, Miss Lawrence. If I had worn my armor, I would not be here at all, but would still be trapped beneath the surface of the pond, the curricle riding on my back."

His dark eyes then raked her up and down as if he had weighed her up and found her sadly lacking. He took two steps before saying, "If you'll excuse me now, please? I think I shall be returning to my castle to have a tapestry commissioned commemorating my latest heraldic deed."

Then Mary was left quite alone, her mouth hanging open, as she watched Tristan being led away, Dexter's arm draped protectively about his shoulders while two dozen or more hangers-on trailed along behind.

"Never mind her, Tris," she heard Dexter say. "Women don't understand these things like we men do. All they can think of is us getting our heads broken or something. She didn't really mean anything by it, I'm sure of it."

Mary couldn't quite hear Tristan's answer, but she certainly understood the tone. She had opened her silly mouth and put herself firmly back into Tristan Rule's black books. Now he would never see her as anything more than Sir Henry's ill-mannered ward—and as a possible threat to England's security.

He'd never see her as a woman. And that made Mary sad . . . it made her very sad indeed.

CHAPTER EIGHT

"He's doing this just to infuriate me, you know. Oh, don't shake your head, Jennie, for you know I'm right."

Jennie Wilde was hard-pressed to conceal her smile as she watched Mary flutter about the Bourne drawing room like a kite in a stiff breeze. "Inviting you to share a theater box with the Grand Duchess Catherine of Oldenburg infuriates you, Mary? And what, pray, would make you happy? Having him appear at the theater with some other young woman on his arm?"

"Yes—No! Oh, Jennie, you know what I mean. It's like that Lorenzo Dow fellow said: 'You will be damned if you do—And you will be damned if you don't.' "

"I believe the man was speaking about religion, Mary, not a festive night at Covent Garden," Jennie supplied, tongue-in-cheek. "But I cannot see how you can turn a simple invitation into something even remotely devious."

Mary flitted about a moment or two more, then came to roost on the settee across from where her friend was reclining at her ease. "The grand duchess is rewarding Tristan's courage in stopping that curricle last week—all the town knows it. Her theater box will be the cynosure of all eyes for the entire evening. And Tristan knows

I would sooner shave my head and wear rags than miss such a spectacle."

"I understand what you are saying so far, Mary." Jennie nodded, picking up her knitting. "But where does the revenge come in?"

Mary rolled her eyes heavenward, unable to believe that Jennie—who was usually so awake on all suits—could be so dense. "For goodness sake, Jennie, Tristan *knows* if I appear as his companion for such a public display that everyone and his wife will have us as good as married!"

Jennie laid down her knitting to peer intently into Mary's worried green eyes. "And to think, my dear, the main presentation of the evening is to be an allegorical festival entitled 'The Grand Alliance.' My goodness, anyone would think the authors had you and Tristan in mind, rather than England and our allies." Shaking her head in mock dismay, she went on: "Perhaps you have been trotting too hard, Mary. Really, the ideas you get into your head amaze even me!"

Mary was not so self-involved that she could not see the humor in Jennie's words. Wrinkling up her pert little nose, she retorted, "Oh, pooh—I guess I am going a bit overboard, aren't I?" Then she became serious once again. "But, Jennie, I already told you how horridly I behaved to Tristan last week after he'd made his daring rescue. Surely he can't be *rewarding* me for such a terrible attack on his character? Have I told you that he has come to visit Aunt Rachel and Sir Henry nearly every day without so much as inquiring about me? Now, does that sound like the man is perishing for the sight of me—or that he would be desirous of my company? No," she answered for herself, "it does not. He knows full well how he has curtailed my social life, and he is purposely using this invitation to throw yet another damper on my fun."

"I think I'm beginning to get the headache," Jennie mused, lifting one hand to her temple.

"That's what Aunt Rachel says every time I bring up the subject," Mary responded, shaking her head. "You all think I'm reading entirely too much into this invitation, don't you? Very well, I'll accept it. But remember this, Jennie, I do so only under duress."

"And because you wish to sit beside the grand duchess at the theater and queen it over all society for an evening," Jennie added facetiously, picking up her knitting once more. "Look at this, Mary. It's a sweater for Christopher—he looks so well in blue, you know, just like his father." Resting the half-done sweater once more in her lap, Jennie closed her eyes. "Lord, how I miss that little scrap of mischief. We're off to Bourne at the end of the week, thank goodness. I vow I don't believe I can wait to have Christopher dribbling down the front of my best gown again!"

Jennie had Mary's full attention now. "Leaving! But—but you can't! Tristan's still snooping about in my past like some Bow Street runner. I may yet need your Ben to help me throw a rub in his way."

"I've already discussed that with Kit and Lucy," Jennie told her soothingly. "Ben is to remain in London along with our grooms, Tiny and Goliath. Lucy has agreed to house them and keep them at your disposal if the need should arise."

"Tiny and Goliath?" Mary questioned. "I don't believe I've—er—had the pleasure."

Jennie grinned happily, always enjoying a conversation that had to do with the successful conclusion of one of her campaigns to find niches for every stray who crossed her path. She then gifted Mary with a full description of her valuable, if a bit outrageous, grooms—a description that cheered Mary more than a little bit as she and her maid departed the Wilde town house and instructed the coachman to drive them to Bond Street and the modiste Mary knew to be capable of producing the most suitable gown for a gala evening at the theater.

To say that Tristan Rule was not enjoying his current status of hero would be reading far too much into his title of Ruthless, for Baron Rule was as human as the next man when it came to flattery.

Oh, he might have made a fine outward show of disdain and disinterest concerning the glowing reports of his bravery in the daily newspapers; he may have declined to purchase any of the flattering cartoons circulating about the city; he may even have tossed Dexter Rutherford out on his ear when that enraptured youth showed up on his doorstep dressed head to toe in black in emulation of his hero, but that did not mean he wished everyone would just forget the incident and let him get on with his life.

To be truthful, after long years spent laboring for his country in secrecy never thinking of public reward—Tristan was finding the adulation of his peers to be comforting indeed. His reputation as Ruthless Rule added much to the stories now circulating throughout the metropolis, and Tristan found it a source of no little amusement to hear that he was personally responsible for military victories and governmental coups that would have necessarily placed him in three European capitals at the same time.

Not the least of the accolades accorded him was the personal invitation of the grand duchess to share her box at the Theatre Royal, Covent Garden on the evening of June 13. That the grand duchess was using him to draw some of the attention away from the Prince Regent, whom she cordially loathed, was not lost on Tristan, but as he also had little love for "Swellfoot," this did not dampen his enthusiasm.

The icing on the cake—although Rule would not have phrased it so—was the grand duchess's gracious inclusion of personal guests of Tristan's own choosing in the party. Even now, as he sauntered down Bond Street—out on the strut, as Dexter and his cronies would have so inelegantly put it—Tristan could not help but smile at the look of confusion mixed with snippets of suspicion and ill-concealed delight in Mary's eyes when he first offered his invitation. Indeed, her consternation in the face of snipping off her own nose to spite her face went a long way toward Tristan's getting a little of his own back for Mary's insults the day of the Venetian breakfast.

And now, tucked securely in his waistcoat pocket, lay that same Miss Lawrence's handwritten acceptance of his invitation that had been delivered directly after luncheon. After a visit to his tailor—and a very much out-of-character interest in every aspect of the construction of a new suit of evening clothes—Tristan went on his way to a meeting with Lords Bourne and Thorpe, to ask their help in the investigation of Mary Lawrence's background.

"Here he is now, Julian," Kit called out, nudging his friend in the ribs, "the man all London has taken to its breast. How condescending of him to agree to be seen with us in public. It will do our combined consequence no little harm to be seen with the Redoubtable Rule, you know. Should we bow, do you think?"

Tristan could not help but overhear, which he was meant to do. "Redoubtable? That's one I haven't heard," he said as he fell into step with his two friends. "Julian?" he asked, turning his head to address Lord Thorpe. "Have you nothing to add—or has Kit poked enough fun at me to suffice?"

Julian Rutherford may have had more than his share of starch for a great deal of his life, but association with his madcap wife, Lucy, had made serious inroads on his hauteur. "My dear fellow," he drawled now, taking Tristan's elbow, "far be it from me to poke fun at you at your expense. By the by, is it true you will be performing your recent stunt twice nightly at Astley's, where the outlay of a trifling three shillings will allow all the ragtags and lowlife's to *ooh* and *aah* at your magnificence?"

By now they had walked as far as St. James's and were entering Boodle's, where they had planned to share a few bottles before the dinner hour. Tristan did not respond to Julian's teasing until they were all cozily ensconced around a table at the "dirty" end of the room, as Kit had gone riding earlier and was still clad in his buckskins. "Rumor, my friend, only rumor," he assured him. "I find myself content with putting Miss Mary Lawrence through her paces, actually. Lucy was right, Julian, inviting Miss Lawrence to make up my party for the theater has that lady jumping through the hoops quite in line with my directions."

Julian raised one finely etched eyebrow. "Lucy has been aiding and abetting again, has she? Kit, does that thought rankle with you as much as it does with me?"

Kit, who had given his permission for three of his servants to remain in town at Mary's disposal, moved uncomfortably in his seat for a moment. "Both our ladies seem to be putting their pretty noses into something that is not their business, don't they? Yet, Tris, I must tell you, I cannot be best pleased with that smirk you are wearing at the moment. Right now I believe Miss Lawrence to have been sadly betrayed—considering how she is laboring under the misapprehension that our wives are completely in her camp. Could it be that they have a plan of their own in the works?''

Julian took a sip from his wineglass. "Of course they do, my dear man. I've been hearing wedding bells ever since those two conniving females first set eyes on Tristan and Mary together on the dance floor.''

Now Tristan spoke up. "No, no, Julian, you have it all wrong. Lucy is aiding me in my attempt to uncover the secrets of Miss Lawrence's past, that is all. In a way, you might say she is doing a service to her country.''

Kit choked on his wine at Tristan's gullibility. "Did you hear that, Julian? Your wife's just doin' her duty. Perhaps she'll get a medal. God—to think two little slips like our wives could have succeeded in pulling the wool so firmly over our hero's eyes. Sickens a man, don't it?''

"Are you saying that Jennie and Lucy are still bent on marrying me off?'' Tristan asked, a steely look coming into his eyes.

"Quick, ain't he?'' Kit quipped, taking another drink.

Julian sat back against his chair, one hand to his chin as he considered the thing. On the one hand, Jennie and Lucy were helping Mary in her attempt to confuse and infuriate Tristan, while on the other hand, they were aiding and abetting Tristan in his search into Mary's past. Both ploys were only decoys—with the ladies taking dead-set aim on leading the two unsuspecting souls straight to the altar. "Kit,'' he said at last, kicking the legs of his chair front once more and placing his elbows firmly on the table, "I think we should do our utmost to aid Tristan in his determination to uncover Miss Lawrence's past. What do you say to allowing your servants Ben, Goliath, and Tiny to remain behind with me in London after you return home to Bourne at the end of the week? That way they could be at Tristan's disposal if ever he should need them."

"But—" Kit began, knowing that he had already agreed to leave the three men behind to aid Mary. Then a slow smile played about his lips as he considered the havoc the three servants could cause if they served *both* Tristan and Mary without either of the plotters being the wiser. Oh, Julian, you're a deep one, Kit mused to himself— besides, why should the ladies have all the fun? "I agree totally, Julian," he said at last, keeping his tone as serious as he could make it. "Tristan may have need of their services in case things get sticky."

Tristan, believing things to be falling neatly into place, raised his glass in salute. "Thank you, gentlemen. I should have come to you at the first, and not relied on my scatter-witted cousins. It takes men to sort things out intelligently, doesn't it?"

Julian and Kit merely smiled and lifted their glasses.

CHAPTER NINE

Mary was not the fluttering type, but she gave a grand imitation of that empty-headed sort of female in the days preceding the theater party. From spending three hours in front of her mirror arranging and rearranging her hair in different styles—to the frustration of her maid, who knew a hopeless case when she saw it, and Mary in a severe topknot was a hopeless sight indeed—to hounding Rachel about matters of protocol and the correct addressing of a grand duchess while seated behind her in a theater box, to badgering Sir Henry into trimming his beloved side whiskers in order to look more top-o'-the-trees, Mary was beginning to wear very thin on everyone's nerves.

Only Kitty was immune, even though she resided in the second guest chamber directly across the hall from all the hustle and bustle. For Kitty was in love, and all she needed or wanted—or, for that matter, acknowledged—in her world was one Dexter Rutherford.

It was, therefore, with great haste and breathless anticipation that she raced down the stairs and into the drawing room when Rachel told her—with an air of abstraction due to Mary's latest bout of hysterics over uneven hems—that she had a morning visitor.

Kitty skidded to a halt inside the doorway, her

smile frozen on her lips, and whispered, "Oh, Gemini, it's you!"

"Not who you were expecting, am I, sis?" the puce-clad exquisite drawled as he minced across the room to take his sister's limp hand and raise it to his lips. "I hear you and that Rutherford dolt are about to make a match of it. Dare I remind you that you needs must gain my permission before launching yourself on the sea of marital bliss?"

"Oh, Gemini, Jerome, say you won't deny us!" Kitty pleaded, her large blue eyes already filling with tears. "After all, it was you who introduced Dex to me."

"And me who got you situated so cozily in this nice, deep gravy boat, if you'll recall," her brother added, taking out a scented handkerchief and lifting it to his nose. "And what I have been so magnanimous in giving I can just as easily take away—can't I, puss?"

"You—you wouldn't!" Kitty exclaimed, feeling her knees grow weak. She looked at her sibling, so alike in looks and yet so vastly different in temperament, and realized that, yes, he would. "What—what do you want, Jerome? Surely it won't be like that last time? Surely you won't ask me to *steal* for you again? Oh, Gemini, I think I'm going to faint."

Jerome pushed Kitty down into a chair and leaned over her, his hands pressed on either side of the cushions next to her head. "You're not going to faint, you silly chit, you're going to listen. I've taken care of you so far, haven't I? Now forget that little episode in Bath and concentrate on what I'm about to tell you."

Kitty listened, her hopes for a future with Dexter Rutherford by her side crumbling into dust at her feet as Jerome outlined his plans.

* * *

According to the program clutched in her nerveless fingers, the Monday evening production at Covent Garden was "in compliment to our illustrious visitors," which included Czar Alexander of Russia and King Frederick of Prussia, among others. To Mary, however, it felt as if the entire evening had been staged in order to try her endurance—not to mention her patience.

Her endurance had held up bravely under the strain, although it had made serious dents in Rachel's usually unflappable demeanor when it was discovered at the last possible minute that the flowers Rule had sent clashed badly with Mary's gown.

It was Mary's *patience* that was in sore need of reinforcement—and had been ever since Tristan showed up on the doorstep and Sir Henry announced that he and Rachel would travel together to the theater, leaving "the young couple to enjoy themselves without us old people around to throw a damper on things."

"Oh, Gemini, how romantic!" Kitty gushed, showing her first real animation in days, so that Mary could not find it in her heart to tell the silly girl that it was not romantic in the least—it was depressing.

Before her maid could settle her light shawl around her bare shoulders, for one fleeting moment Mary thought of sacrificing herself to lending comfort to Kitty, who had decided to remain at home that evening since Dexter was at the moment paying his twice-yearly duty call on his Great-Aunt Felicity in Brighton. But the feeling, never heartfelt, faded without regret when Mary caught sight of herself in the foyer mirror and realized that the stunning result of two weeks of dedication should not be left to molder away at home. It would be criminal to deprive the world of the sight of her new, soft-as-butter yellow silk gown because she objected to riding in the same coach with Tristan Rule.

But now, now as she sat in the grand duchess's theater box, awaiting that lady's arrival, Mary was having second thoughts. Besides being situated at the very rear of the box where none, save the servant handing around lemonade, could appreciate her splendor, Mary had already crossed swords with Tristan twice during the short drive—and lost to him both times.

It seemed that, while Mary had busied herself with gathering her ensemble for the evening, Tristan had been engaged in his favorite project— digging into Mary's supposedly illicit past.

They had not been in the coach above a minute before he had—by the simple means of declaring her to be five and twenty if she was a day— goaded her into telling him her correct age of eighteen. Within ten minutes he had the name of her first governess from her after twitting her that he had discovered information that led him to believe she had been left on some orphanage front doorstep with a note pinned to her nappy.

"Are you comfortable?" Tristan asked now as he seated himself beside her. "Once the grand duchess arrives, I'm sure we can secure chairs farther front, but I would not like to push myself forward now only to be asked to move to the rear."

Mary's head turned slowly, oh so slowly, in his direction, taking in his elegant dress and well-groomed appearance. "Move the hero of Richmond Park to the rear, my lord? Surely you jest! Why, I do believe there would be a riot in the pit if anyone dared do such a shabby thing."

Tristan had the good sense to drop the subject, for he knew himself not to be totally innocent of enjoying his new fame. Feigning an interest in the programme he held, he commented, "They're putting on a revival of *Richard Coeur de Lion*, with Mr. Barrymore as Blondel. Are you much impressed by historical romances of this type, Miss Lawrence, or are you looking forward to the farce *Dead Alive*?"

"I look forward to meeting the grand duchess, sir," Mary replied icily. "Nothing else could have induced me to spend even a moment in your company, as you well know." Drat it all anyway, she fumed inwardly, did he have to lean so close to her ear to speak to her? He was turning her insides to mush!

"And I would endure the grand duchess and all the crowned heads for a moment spent at *your* side," Tristan whispered into her ear, holding to his resolve to keep her confused by romancing her while persisting with his investigation of her past. The only thing that surprised him was that, although he considered his wooing to be a duty he owed his country, he was finding the project had personal rewards he had not considered, one of them being the opportunity to be close to the most beautiful creature in the theater that night. If only he could believe Mary had dressed with such care in order to impress him, he would have surprised himself by being the happiest of men—but his saner self told him otherwise.

The next few minutes passed in strained silence, Mary refusing to answer Tristan's latest sally, and as the grand duchess arrived only a moment before the musicians began tuning up their instruments, imperiously commanding Tristan and Mary to take seats on either side of her, there was no further opportunity for conversation.

Mary could now see from her clearer vantage point that the theater was full almost to overflowing, and she could barely make out Sir Henry and Aunt Rachel in a box near the stage. The royal box was full to bursting, the Prince Regent and his entourage, which included the Czar, bustling into their seats just as the curtain was drawn up to the singing of "God Save the King."

Tristan and Mary joined the chorus, as did Prinny and, to the patrons' pleasure, the czar. The sovereigns seated themselves once more and Mary was just about to follow suit when suddenly there broke out a round of shouting and applause, and the entire audience turned as one to look at the Princess of Wales's box, where Caroline, Prinny's estranged wife, was waving merrily to the crowd.

"Here we go," Tristan half whispered, and Mary saw that the grand duchess, far from being appalled, was laughing quite heartily at the Regent's dilemma.

Caroline was resplendent in diamonds and wearing a black wig—hardly flattering, but certainly eye-catching, which was most probably her intent. The czar—whom rumor said had taken to lecturing the Prince Regent on the advisability of reconciling with his wife—stood and bowed in Caroline's direction while everyone held their breath to see what would happen next.

Prinny pushed his not inconsiderable bulk to a standing position and gave a deep, graceful bow—as if acknowledging the cheering of the crowd that had lately taken to hissing him whenever he rode his closed carriage through the streets. Not once did he look in his wife's direction, and at last that woman had the good grace to sit down.

"Hummph!" The grand duchess sniffed. "We do not like him," she said quite audibly, leaving no one in confusion as to whom she meant.

Tristan, who privately thought the Regent to be a sorry sight indeed, found himself bristling at the insult. How dare the woman dislike the heir to the throne, no matter what his failings? He actually opened his mouth to defend the man, when Mary's slight negative shake of her head forestalled him.

She was right, of course. It wouldn't do to create an incident. Tristan subsided into his seat as King Richard, played by someone named Sinclair, took center stage. It was only as the presentation was drawing to a close that he realized he had deferred to Mary's judgment—something he had made it a rule never to do. Was he getting soft, losing his edge? Or, he mused ruefully, was Mary gaining some sort of power over him?

He sneaked a look in her direction as she sat forward in her chair, clearly caught up in the finale, and watched as the tip of her tongue darted out to moisten her slightly parted lips. Suddenly he wished the grand duchess, the czar, Prinny and his soiled princess, and all the rest of the world at the bottom of the deepest sea.

When the intermission was announced, he fairly catapulted himself out of his chair and over to Mary's side, requesting her company in the corridor. Without giving her a chance to decline, he prized her out of her seat by the elbow and pushed her in front of him until they had squeezed through the doorway and into the still fairly empty hallway.

"Really, sir," Mary protested, wresting her elbow out of his grasp, "you have the manners of a ruffian. You did not even tarry to inquire as to whether or not our hostess wished to accompany us."

"Hang the harridan," Tris was pushed to say, looking about quickly to locate a private bench where the two of them could talk without being overheard. "Here," he said, motioning his head toward a shallow alcove on the other side of the corridor, "come with me."

"Aren't you going to bring me some lemonade?" Mary asked once they had been seated as Tristan sat stiffly and as far away from her as the length of the bench would allow. "You're supposed to ask me if I wish some refreshments."

"Hang the refreshments!" Tristan nearly shouted, causing more than one interested head to turn in their direction. More softly, he added, "I mean, we already had some in the box, didn't we? Wasn't that enough? Besides, I want to talk to you."

"More questions, my lord?" Mary asked tightly. "Haven't you gouged enough information from me for one night? When are you going to realize that you are chasing shadows that simply do not exist? I know my past; Sir Henry knows my past—and neither of us fears discovery will put England in danger. Really, sir, you refine too much on the ability of one frail female to—"

"And *hang* your dubious past!" Rule cut in ruthlessly. "I am more interested in your impact upon *me* at the moment!"

"My impact upon—" Mary began wonderingly, and then she raised her gloved hands slowly to her mouth as her feminine logic cut straight to the heart of the matter. "Oh, Tris, you are infatuated with me! This is famous!"

"I am not!" Tris denied hotly. "You are nothing more than yet another project I have undertaken in the best interests of my country."

Mary shook her head, her auburn curls dancing about delightfully. "Oh no, you are infatuated with me. Lucy and Jennie said you were, but I didn't believe them. Oh, those two—I must give them my congratulations, their intuitions were correct."

Tristan looked about him, hoping against hope

they were not attracting a crowd. "Will you be quiet for a moment?" he nearly begged. "This is serious. I find myself doubting my own conclusions—even my motives—when it comes to you. I'm unaccustomed to doubt, as it has never plagued me before in my career. I've always been able to rely on my instincts to guide me. Now it— it's like I'm stumbling about in a dense fog, trying to feel my way." He took a deep breath and said heavily, "I'm thinking of withdrawing from public service, telling Sir Henry my services are no longer available."

Mary pressed a hand to her breast. "Because you find yourself infatuated with me?"

"Damn it woman, I'm *not* infatuated with you!" he fairly hissed. "I must just be tired, and this last investigation has proved to be my undoing. What I need to know from you now is: if I agree to cease my investigation and retire to my estate and my badly neglected duties there, will you at least be honest with me so that I can be sure once and for all that your past presents no danger to Sir Henry?"

Leave London? Retire to his estate? Mary's heart did a little flip-flop in her breast at the thought. All she had to do to be rid of Tristan Rule was to tell him the truth—tell him her father had been French and that Sir Henry was worried her late father's old enemies might try to revenge themselves upon his daughter—and he would go out of her life forever.

A scant month ago this thought would have served to raise her into the boughs with delight. Now, she realized with quickening pulse, it was the very last thing she desired. He swore he wasn't infatuated with her—not that the man would know what infatuation was if it reared up and kicked him in the face—but she couldn't believe it, refused to believe it.

Look at him, she told herself, gazing tenderly into his confused, handsome face. He's so dear when he isn't scowling. For all his exploits, all his importance to the government, he is almost child-like in his experience in the real world—in *my* world. In just the same way he is learning that all is not black and white, that shades of gray exist everywhere. He is beginning to learn about the stirrings of the heart. And *I* am the first woman to have touched him romantically, for all his heart-breaking good looks and dashing reputation.

Mary began to feel the power women have always felt when they recognized the hold their frail fingers could place on a man's heart. Tell him everything now? Free him to go hide at his estate until his defenses were restored to their former iron-hard strength? She'd rather go back to Sussex and her rustic keepers!

"I repeat for the very last time, my lord," she said finally, "there is no great secret about me. I am Sir Henry's ward—no more, no less. If you wish to run away from a mere female who has proved too much for the great Ruthless Rule, it is not I who shall shed a tear as you ride off. But if you wish to stay, you shall have to do your own sleuthing. I shall not gift you with any clues."

So saying, she rose to return to the grand duchess's box for the farce. Just as she slipped into her chair, with Rule dutifully, if a bit belliger-ently, holding it steady for her, she whispered, "And you are too infatuated!"

CHAPTER TEN

Mary was still in a most jovial mood the morning following her visit to Covent Garden, and with good reason. The sight of Tristan Rule in a temper, a frequent yet—as she knew herself to be the reason for his chagrin—enjoyable spectacle, had served to lift her spirits throughout the remainder of the theater party, and his grumbling and mumbling as he fairly raced her home through the streets had placed the perfect cap upon the evening.

She was flattered by his obvious infatuation with her, as so correctly predicted by Jennie and Lucy, especially considering the fact that she had at last acknowledged her own feelings in the matter. Tristan Rule, despite her initial protests concerning the way he had cut out all her other beaux by his outrageous behavior, had become very dear to her.

Infuriating he might be, but he was also, as Rachel had said, unfailingly loyal and completely sincere. Indeed, Mary's retort to Rachel that she once had a puppy with the same attributes came fairly close to the mark when it came to Mary's interpretations of Rule's charms. She considered him to be very puppylike beneath his bristly exterior, and had decided he held the proverbial heart of gold hidden deep within the stern, even aggressive man he showed the world.

That Mary found Tristan to be adorable—the exact word she had used to describe him in her private journal—would have sent everyone who knew Rule into whoops of laughter. The world knew him only by the face he presented to them— a hotheaded though valuable man's man who was about as "cuddly" as a prickly pear.

Either Mary was blinded by infatuation herself, or she was far more intuitive than any woman had ever been when it came to solving the enigma of Tristan Rule—even she couldn't really be sure. She only knew that Tristan refused to acknowl- edge the one thing she knew to be fact: he was infatuated with her!

But infatuation was a far step from love, and Mary knew her own mind well enough to realize that it was his love that she wanted. She had been delighted by her ability to send him into a flutter with her teasing, but she knew that she'd soon catch cold if she persisted in pointing out his— as he must consider it to be—failing. And letting him see how she felt about him would be the best way to send him helter-skelter to the hinterlands and his precious estates in fear for his life.

No, the only way to keep Tristan in town long enough to convince him that he could not live without her was to continue heaping fuel on the fires of his suspicion. For that reason she had sent her maid to the Rutherford stables with a note directing Tiny and Goliath to be outside Sir Henry's kitchen door at midnight, ready to serve as her protectors while she set about laying yet another false trail for Tristan to follow.

Of course, setting false trails only worked if Tristan were aware that she was laying them, which is where Kitty came into the affair—Kitty and her devoted swain, Dexter.

Having asked a servant to tell Miss Toland that

Miss Lawrence requested her company in the drawing room, Mary now sat awaiting that young lady's arrival, still trying without much luck to erase the happy smile that had been with her since Tristan's farewell at the front door the night before. He had been adorably flustered, Mary reflected now, as he stood there, so clearly torn between shaking her hand and crushing her against him in a tight embrace, that he had ended up by lifting her hand to his lips and nearly kissing his own fingers by mistake before backing down the steps to trip clumsily on the flagway as he forgot to watch where he was going. Ah, he was such a dear, she sighed, raising the back of her hand to her cheek, as if holding his kiss against herself.

"Mary? Mary! Oh, Gemini, I'm sorry! I do believe I startled you," Kitty apologized, hesitating in the doorway as if she were about to flee to her chamber in disgrace. "I'm such a bother, aren't I? My brother Jerome always says I tippity-toe on cat's feet, scaring him half out of his mind every time I come into a room."

Mary looked up to see Kitty standing in a puddle of sunshine, her pale golden hair making her resemble nothing so much as an innocent angel, and could not help but wonder to herself how the good Lord stood it, being surrounded by so much naive sweetness. Not that she didn't like Kitty, for she did—very much—but Mary needed a bit more spice in her life, a bit more unpredictability. She smiled at her own thoughts—a bit more Tristan, she could have said.

"Nonsense, Kitty," she told the girl, patting the place beside her, encouraging Kitty to join her on the settee. "I was lost in a daydream, that's all."

Kitty nodded as if she understood, as she had been guilty of daydreaming herself, what with

Dexter due back in town any moment. "It must have been above all things wonderful to be at the theater last night. Miss Gladwin told me all about it this morning over breakfast."

"Yes," Mary agreed, "it certainly was wonderful, though I still can't understand why she and Uncle Henry declined Tristan's invitation at the last minute and chose to watch the performance from the box Uncle rented at the beginning of the Season."

Kitty blushed hotly and lowered her head. "Oh, Gemini, Mary, can't you guess? They wanted you and Tristan to be *alone*. Wasn't that sweet of them?"

Two things occurred to Mary then, the first being that she must make a point of being very nice to Sir Henry for the rest of the day. The second thought was much more selfish—as she realized she had certainly chosen her vehicle well —for Kitty Toland couldn't keep a secret if her life depended on it.

"Yes, well, Kitty," Mary said now, lowering her eyelashes a bit as she found it hard to lie directly into such an innocent, trusting face. "About Tristan—it seems I have this . . . er . . . *problem*."

Kitty leaned forward eagerly, glad to be considered worthy of Mary's confidences.

Dexter, still clad in his travel dirt, ran Tristan to earth late that same afternoon just as the man was stepping out of Gentleman Jackson's Boxing Saloon, and rushed up to take his arm. "Tris, I have to talk to you!" Dexter imparted with uncharacteristic seriousness.

"My goodness, Dex, what nettle has gotten into your breeches?" Tristan teased, feeling much better now that he had bashed at least one of Jackson's underlings in his effort to work out the frustrations caused by yet another long, sleepless night. "Don't tell me you and your little Incomparable are having troubles—and don't think you are about to recommence being my shadow if you are no longer to be playing the lovebird. People were beginning to talk, you know, and I have enough on my plate right now without that!"

Dexter pokered up stiffly at this double insult. "Miss Toland and I are enjoying our customary felicitous relationship, sir," he intoned heavily, "and I would consider it a kindness if you would leave off poking fun at the woman I love."

Tristan stopped in his tracks. "Good God, did I do that?" he asked wonderingly. "And here I thought I was complimenting her good judgment —for casting such a looby as you aside could only be applauded as the action of a discerning female. There," he ended, clapping Dexter bracingly on the back, "have I succeeded in vindicating myself regarding the merits of your Miss Toland?"

"Yes, blister it, Tris, you have," Dexter countered, confusion written all over his face, "but now I do believe I'll have to call you out for your insult to me! Yet if I do that, I really would be guilty of being the stupidest person in nature."

Rule threw back his head and laughed aloud, feeling better and better as each moment passed. He really enjoyed Dexter's company, for the younger man's clear, if rather limited, outlook on life was a delight to witness.

The pair walked on until they espied a small tavern and Tristan suggested they step inside to share a bird and a bottle, which suited Dexter to a cow's thumb, as he had pressing business with Rule that he had momentarily forgotten—business that would surely serve to remove that genial smile from the man's lips.

Once they had been served, Dexter leaned forward in his chair, ready to impart his new-found knowledge, but then, realizing that he was in the most direct line of fire if Tristan decided to explode, he leaned back again and nervously cleared his throat a time or two before speaking. "Tristan . . . um . . . Tris, I happened to stop by Sir Henry's this afternoon to pay a call on Miss Toland and . . . um . . . *I say*, man, that's a devilish fine cravat! Do you think you could have your man instruct mine in the way of it?"

Tristan, who had tied the thing haphazardly himself after his stint in the boxing ring and knew himself to be looking casual, to put it politely, narrowed his dark eyes and measured the man sitting across from him. "Spit it out, Dex. There's something sticking in your craw and I'd say it's about to choke you."

Dexter was all admiration. "How'd you do that, Tris? Julian does it too—always did—reads me like an open book. It's a good thing I don't need to be devious, as I sure don't seem to have the head for it, do I?"

"Nor the face," Rule supplied with a grin. "Now out with it—are you in need of someone to bail you out of the River Tick? I thought you had given up gaming in those hells."

"Haven't touched the dice more than twice since I met Miss Toland," Dexter swore earnestly. "Besides, it doesn't have to do with me at all. It's Miss Lawrence."

Suddenly Tristan, who had been listening with only half an ear, was all attention. "Mar—Miss Lawrence? Is she all right? Was there an accident? You took your bloody sweet time telling me—" Rule was already out of his chair and heading for the door.

"She's fine!" Dexter called out, stopping Rule in his tracks. "At least she is now. It's later on tonight that worries me."

"Tonight?" Tristan repeated, numbly slipping

back into his chair. "She's promised to Lady Jersey's this evening." At the sight of Dexter's raised eyebrows, he continued rather sheepishly: "Sir Henry keeps me informed of her whereabouts —in all innocence, I assure you."

"Of course he does. Of course it is," Dexter agreed, grinning widely. "Nothing at all out of the way about a thing like that."

"Julian should have strangled you in your cot," Tristan said, not pleased to have been found out. "Now tell me why Miss Lawrence could be in trouble tonight before I do Julian's job for him. I assure you, I have experience enough to make the procedure relatively swift and painless."

Running a nervous finger inside the front of his cravat, as if to reassure himself his valet had left him adequate breathing space, Dexter made short work out of his explanation.

It seemed that Kitty had confided in him—in deepest confidence, Tristan was to understand— that Mary had a secret assignation shortly after midnight in Green Park. The only reason Mary had confided in Kitty was so that she would agree to accompany her home early from Lady Jersey's when Mary pleaded the headache. That way Mary would be able to sneak out of the house in time to meet "her tormentor" in the park.

"Her 'tormentor'?" Tristan questioned, his agile mind already deciding that Mary was indeed the victim of some sort of blackmail.

Dexter was nodding his head vigorously, happy to be done with his end of the mission, and grateful that Tristan hadn't taken it into his head to slay the messenger who had brought him the bad news. If Rule wished to believe that pack of nonsense, it wasn't up to him to convince him otherwise—even if Dexter did believe that Mary's appointment was in reality a romantic assignation. After all, what sort of deep intrigue could involve anyone like Mary Lawrence?

"You weren't to know," Dexter then volunteered, as he had never learned to leave well enough alone. "Kitty specifically told me that when she confided her fears in me. Not that I paid her any attention—after giving my solemn word that I'd breathe not a syllable about it to you— seeing as how you work for Sir Henry, sort of, don't you, and should be most concerned lest any scandal come to his ward over some fortune-hunting Romeo."

Dexter later told his friend, Bertie Sandover, that it was then that he first swore he could see smoke rising out of Ruthless Rule's ears. "You think she's eloping with some other man?" Tristan had accused, his strong, lean fingers clutching the table edge in a death grip. "You think that's why Mary was so adamant that I above anyone else was not to know about her plans for the evening?"

"Kitty told me I had been chosen to waylay you in the card room or somewhere until Miss Lawrence could effect her departure from Lady Jersey's," Dexter squeaked in his own defense. "Plain as the nose on your face that she don't want you poking about in her business. Now, Tris—" he warned feebly as Rule gave a low growl.

"You're a few bricks shy of a load, Dex, do you know that?" Tristan gritted through clenched teeth, not knowing what had made him the angrier: Mary's assignation that evening or Dexter's assumption that she was meeting another man. "And stop sliding down in that chair; you'll soon be on the floor! Pull yourself together, man, or you'll be no help to me at all."

"You want me to help you?" Dexter asked, swallowing hard on a gulp. "I thought you wanted to *kill* me."

Tristan called out to the serving wench to bring another bottle to the table. "No, no," he assured the younger man, trying his best to remain calm and make his plans carefully. "After all, if I kill you now, you won't be able to corner me in the card room this evening, will you?"

Mary had been correct in her reading of Kitty's character. When it came to keeping other people's secrets, Kitty Toland showed a lamentable lack of dependability. This worked very much to Mary's advantage when it came to having Tristan informed of her plans for the evening.

It did not, however, work in quite the same way when it came to having Jerome Toland gifted with the same information.

"Did I do right to tell you, Jerry?" Kitty asked her brother fearfully as she watched him pace back and forth across Sir Henry's morning-room carpet. "You said I must keep my eyes and ears open and tell you anything that seemed the least important, although, oh, Gemini, I can't see how Mary's little indiscretion can serve to help you. Surely you don't plan to break into her rooms tonight while she is gone and steal her jewelry, like you did that time in—"

"I told you to blank that memory from your mind, you ridiculous chit!" Jerome interrupted, still gnawing on the side of his thumb as he turned the information he had just learned over in his mind. Actually, he had hoped to insinuate Kitty into some peer's household with just such thievery in mind, but once he learned of Sir Henry's important role in the government, he had revised his plans to include the selling of information to certain persons he knew who were still championing Napoleon's cause. Now he had this new kettle of fish handed to him.

"Will you promise now not to interfere with Dexter's and my plans?" Kitty, emboldened by the deathless love she bore her Dex, dared to ask. "You said if I helped you this one last time, you would agree to the match."

Jerome headed for the door, clearly preoccupied. "We'll see, puss, we'll see," he promised vaguely before quitting the room. "Just do your part tonight like the lady asked you, and remember—you're just as guilty as I am, so *keep your mouth shut about my past!*"

CHAPTER ELEVEN

It had all been so easy—so ridiculously easy. She knew she was right to have counted on Kitty to spill the soup. Mary was convinced Kitty and Dexter had all but drawn Lord Rule a diagram of her plans for the evening. Dexter's maneuvering of Tristan into the card room had certainly lacked for subtlety, but then Tristan's transparent willingness to be led away from his customary pillar-bracing stance at the edge of the ballroom had caused Mary to wonder how he had ever gotten such a reputation for spying—an occupation that she assumed must take a certain talent for subterfuge.

But no matter. It was just striking midnight and she was going to be late if she didn't soon succeed in sticking her unruly mass of hair up inside the oversized toque Ben had supplied her with that afternoon. Really, she thought ruefully as she shrugged herself into the long, shapeless black coat he had told her was part of the customary dress of young apprentices in the city, Ben may have many talents, but an eye for fashion certainly isn't one of them.

After looking at herself one more time in the mirror—seeing a slim, out-at-the-elbows youth dressed in straight loose trousers that went halfway down to her ankles (now shapeless in thick woolen socks and heavy black shoes) and a loose, open-necked blouse whose limp ruffle somewhat hid her bosom—Mary headed for the servants' stairs, her bedside candle held high to light the way.

Ben met her just outside the kitchen door, startling her as he appeared out of the darkness without a sound to whisper in her ear, "Git yer dew beaters travelin', missy, whilst Oi go tickle up yer shadows fer yer. Oi'll be 'ere waitin' on yer when yers git back, mindin' the store, like."

"Huh?" Mary asked inelegantly, still trying to figure out what "dew beaters" were.

Ben shook his head sadly, wondering just how he, once a first-rate kencracker, had been brought so low. "Please yer to start walking now, Miss, whilst Oi goes to tell Tiny and Goliath yer're on yer way."

Mary gifted him with a grateful smile. "Oh, of course. Thank you, Ben. I'll start moving my dew beaters on the instant."

"Bless yer, missy," Ben whispered gratefully before disappearing once more into the shadows, leaving Mary alone again in the foggy yellow moonlight.

She had already plotted out the shortest way to Green Park, carefully planning her route along the best illuminated streets, but that did not keep her from jumping half out of her skin when a noise from a nearby alleyway reached her just as she had finished congratulating herself for having completed half the journey without incident. "Mad as Bedlam," she told herself aloud, "that's what you are, Mary Lawrence, traveling about the city with only a dwarf and a gentle giant as guardians."

She smiled then as she remembered her first sight of Jennie's two grooms that afternoon at

Lucy's. Tiny, the benevolent giant, resembled nothing more than a huge, black mountain with muscular arms the size of cottage beams, while Goliath, clearly the senior partner in their friendship, stood only as high as her waist. In only a few moments Mary was convinced that, between Tiny's brawn and Goliath's brain, she had nothing to fear during her midnight foray in Green Park.

Besides, she told herself yet again, Tristan is bound to be out here somewhere, skulking behind trees and playing bo-peep in dark doorways, watching every move I make. The thought of Tristan seeing her dressed in such an outlandish costume caused Mary to pause a moment beneath a street lamp to inspect her appearance in a nearby shop window.

Now what's she doing? Lord Rule asked himself as he flattened his body against the side of a building. Poking his head around the corner, he espied her adjusting her toque in a rather rakish tilt. "Plaguey queer time to be primping!" he muttered, wondering yet again (rather like Ben) how he had ever been brought to this pass.

Chancing a quick look behind him, he saw that Tiny and Goliath were still in sight. "Lord," he hissed, "that man is big!" Not that Rule didn't believe himself capable of handling any problems, but Kit had offered his services, and Rule had decided not to take any chances with Mary's welfare. Between the two of them, Tris and Tiny could hold off an army of cutthroats while Goliath led Mary to safety.

Safety. Tristan snorted, disbelief at Mary's naiveté making him shake his head sadly. You'd think she was out strolling the park with her maid at high noon, the way she's just walking along without once looking to see if she's about to be attacked from behind. Lord, if she were to turn around and see Tiny's hulking figure coming up on her out of the fog—*that* would serve to put a period to her shenanigans!

Rule waited until Mary had crossed the street and entered the park before darting across himself to run from tree to tree as she cut deeper into the park, his tall figure bent nearly in half. At last she stopped, looked around her a time or two—all without seeing either Rule or the two servants, who stood not twenty paces away from her in the shrubbery—before removing a folded sheet of paper and placing it carefully in a knothole of the largest tree in the area.

Rule motioned to the servants with a toss of his head, sending Tiny and Goliath back the way they had come as Mary turned for home, while he counted slowly to twenty before crossing to the tree and removing the message Mary had hidden there before he too quit the park.

Standing under the same street lamp Mary had used to check on her appearance, Rule unfolded the note and held it up toward the light. " 'Iz-js duy-typ-zfe jy—' What the bloody hell? It's in *code!*" He lifted his head just in time to see yet another dark-clad figure disappear into the fog. The man the message was intended for? he asked himself, even as he stuffed the paper into his coat and started off at a dead run to capture Mary's "tormentor."

"Nearly two," Mary said aloud, listening for the chiming of the hall clock and wondering what on earth could be keeping Rule. She had returned home and run up the servants' stairs just as fast as her heavy black shoes could carry her, to stand in the window and wave her candle slowly back and forth across the window three times—signaling to

Ben that she was safe in her room, but hoping Rule would take it as more proof of her clandestine activities.

She had then hastily ripped off her clothes and dived into her nightgown, expecting Sir Henry to be calling her downstairs at any moment for a confrontation with her accuser. She had even, as the moments dragged into minutes, sat herself down at her dressing table to arrange her hair becomingly and dab on just a hint of that lovely lip pomade Lucy had loaned her.

So where was Tristan? Mary had counted on him not waiting to decipher her note, had relied on his reputation for action before thought. It just wasn't like him to retire to his rooms and patiently work out the code.

"Oh why, oh why hasn't he come crashing through the front door bellowing like a bull?" she asked herself, pouting. "How like him to be so contrary as to spoil all my fun!"

"What in thunder are you about?" Sir Henry demanded, lowering the pistol he had aimed at the intruder's heart.

Lord Rule, one foot on the floor, the other still hovering on the sill, halted in his progress through Sir Henry's bedchamber window. "I should have remembered, shouldn't I?" Tris answered, pulling himself entirely into the room. "Many's the tale I've heard about you in your younger days." Drawing himself up to his full height, he then bowed. "Sir, your most obedient—"

"Yes, yes, get on with it," Sir Henry prodded, "and spare me any recital of my foolish salad days in the field. I'm just on the sunny side of fifty now, even if my ears and instincts remain good. What brings you here in the middle of the night? More plots to free Napoleon?"

"If only it were, sir," Tristan said, lowering himself into a chair to rest a moment before—his hot blood denying him more than a momentary respite—he sprang to his feet once more. "I can deal with the mundane," he began in a rush, consigning an entire network of dangerous spies and conspirators to the everyday, "but I swear to you, this is beyond me!"

"Prinny?" Ruffton prodded. "A plot to kill him? It'd be the third this month."

Rule shook his head and reached into his pocket to pull out the incriminating paper and hand it to his mentor. "I found this stuck in a tree in Green Park. Your 'ward' put it there this evening, just after midnight."

Sir Henry looked at the paper for a moment like a man who had just been offered a snake, then snapped it from Rule's hand. "What in Hades was Mary doing in Green Park? And how do you know she was?"

"I followed her there," Tristan answered, running a hand through his hair before turning to stare out the window into the darkness.

"Plague take you, Rule, my ward is none of your business! I told you before that your suspicions of her are nothing but a great piece of nonsense. Shadowing her like some sneaking spy—you show a deplorable lack of confidence in me, Rule, and I vow I cannot like that," Sir Henry lectured, hunting the top of his dresser for his reading spectacles.

Tristan whirled to face the older man. "I begin to think we are talking at cross-purposes. Didn't you hear what I said?" he asked, not believing his ears. "Your 'ward'—your 'niece'—went to Green Park tonight to deliver a message to somebody. Whether it was spying or blackmail—aren't you the least concerned for her welfare?"

Sir Henry adjusted his spectacles—the nose-piece almost always pinched, which was why he usually tried to do without—and allowed a small chuckle to escape him. "If I know Mary, and I know her a great deal better than you do, my lad, she had a good reason for doing what she did. She's now down the hall, safely tucked in her bed, I presume?"

"She is," Rule said disgustedly. "Goli—er, my operative assured me of her safety. I could not see her back here myself, as I was too busy chasing down the man for whom she intended the message."

"Showed you a clean pair of heels, did he?" Sir Henry observed, looking up from his work of deciphering Mary's code. "What makes you think this man is involved? Could have been some innocent passerby you scared half out of his wits. Probably won't stop running until he hits John O'Groats. Let's see here—I believe one letter just substitutes for another. Let's try *O* for *Y*."

Rule, a mulish expression on his handsome face, looked at Sir Henry in astonishment. "I can't believe what I'm hearing! God give me patience! How does she do it? How does she constantly manage to pull the wool over everyone's eyes? Well, sir, I am not so easily duped. Either Miss Lawrence is the target of some nefarious scheme or you, sir, have nurtured a viper at your bosom!"

Sir Henry looked up at Rule over his spectacles. "Oh, stop being so damned officious, son. And before you start reading me one of your famous scolds, remember, I already told you that Mary has had a rather unorthodox upbringing. She means no harm, I assure you."

"Don't tell me yet again about how you left her in Sussex with none but rough-and-ready retired army men and half-witted chaperons to tend her,"

Tristan said indignantly. "Tell me instead *why* she was hidden away down in Sussex in the first place."

"*I* for *Z*, *T* for *J*—ah yes, this is really quite elementary." Ruffton raised a hand to shush Rule as he scribbled quickly, crossing out letters and substituting others. "I am not yet in my dotage to be taken in by some green girl," he supplied off-handedly as he worked. "Whatever this message is, I'm sure it's nothing to do with either blackmail or the security of this great nation. You've been pesting her again, I'll wager, and now she's funning you to get some of her own back."

Tristan threw up his hands, not able to believe he had somehow found himself in Bedlam. "That's it? That's all you have to say on the matter? A young, defenseless—not to mention *witless*—girl goes sauntering about London after midnight and you tell me she's only pulling a prank. You *condone* this? You even, by your lighthearted treatment of her, *encourage* such—what is it? Have you broken the code? Sits it serious?"

Sir Henry, who furrowed his brow as the words began to fall into place, now sat back in his chair, his face entirely devoid of expression. "Sit down, son," he said now. "I don't believe I wish to involve Perkins in this if you swoon dead away and I have to get you boosted into my bed."

"I can't believe it," Tristan whispered. "I had all but assured myself of her innocence in any plots against the government. My only concern was that her past might somehow be discovered and used for private gain. But it isn't blackmail, is it? She wasn't in the park paying off some tormentor, was she?"

"Oh, I don't know," Ruffton opined, trying hard not to smile. "I begin to think she has paid him off quite as much as he deserved. Would you care to hear the contents of the message?"

Rule drew himself up to his full height. "Sir, I cannot, no matter what my personal feelings for either you or Miss Lawrence, shirk my duty to my country. If the contents of that message are vital to the government, you cannot make me hide what I know. Perhaps it would be better if you were to withhold the knowledge from me."

Now Sir Henry did let go with a small chuckle. "How very—er—*noble* of you, Tristan, to sacrifice England's safety for Mary."

"And for you, sir," Tris added, indeed feeling a bit noble.

"Of course, for me. It is a comfort to know I have someone willing to commit treason to shield me from the follies of my ward. But before you trot off to the country to fall on your sword in some wood, will you kindly oblige me by sitting down and listening to what the message has to say?"

Rule sat himself down, cleared his throat, and motioned for Sir Henry to proceed.

And proceed Sir Henry did. "It begins: 'With apologies to Little Jack Horner—

"My Lord Tristan Rule vows *he* is no fool;
At Deduction he's top of his *class.*
Swift judgments he makes, never fearing mistakes,
While quite closely resembling an *ass.*

"The Ruthless milord has accused Ruffton's ward
Of both spying and lying as *well.*
In her life he does pry, asking why-why-why *why*?
While the lady consigns him to *hell.*

"The ward's not confessin'; thinkin' Rule needs
    a lesson
That will greatly his confidence *rattle.*
So a ruse she plays out, meant to put him to rout,
And he hotfoots to Ruffton to *tattle.*

"Now Redoubtable Rule (obtuse but not cruel),
Too late recognizes her *gambit*.
He's been chasing his tail, for she's laid a false
  trail;
Rues he hotly: 'She's bested me, *dammit.*' "

Mary would have looked at Tristan and privately thought he looked endearingly boyish in his embarrassment. It will never be known what Sir Henry would have thought, for he could not bring himself to look at the young man without fear of breaking into his first fit of the giggles since his years at Eton.

When at last Sir Henry assured himself that he could speak without betraying his enjoyment of his ward's sense of humor, he offered to do anything he could to ease Lord Rule's mind further on the subject of Mary Lawrence.

"I would have you lock her in her chamber, but I doubt it will answer the purpose," Tristan observed with unusual geniality before, his temper at last getting the better of him, he fairly shouted: "Damn it all, Sir Henry, tell me again what a citadel of propriety she is when she swears like a trooper!"

Sir Henry merely shrugged his shoulders. "I told you about her upbringing. Rachel says it is one of my great failings—using pensioned-off soldiers as house servants. But even if I had confined them all to the stables, I fear Mary would have sought them out. Was a bit of a tomboy when I first met her, you know."

But Tristan wasn't listening. He was pacing back and forth on the carpet in a flaming fury, his dark eyes flashing fire. "Why did she feel such a crushing need to stage this charade?—for it's as sure as I'm standing here that this entire evening has been enacted for my benefit. I thought she understood that I no longer believed her to be a spy."

"Ah, but was that enough for you?" Sir Henry asked, twisting the knife a little bit. "Or did you demand that she tell you all about herself—the same way you've been poking and prodding at me with that overly inquisitive nose of yours?"

Tristan slammed his closed fist into his palm. "You won't talk, either of you!"

Sir Henry looked owlishly at Tristan's balled fist. "Do you mean to beat it out of me, then?"

Tristan's anger deflated, just like a balloon when the air is let out, and he sank into a chair, his legs spread out in front of him. "She worries me, Sir Henry. If there's some scandal in her past, someone may try to hurt her with it—or you through her."

Sir Henry pulled up a chair to sit directly in front of the younger man. "Now why don't I believe that my safety—or even that of England's—is your first concern. Mary's past is her concern, you know. Hers and mine. But I'll tell you this much: her parents were old acquaintances of mine, people whose names still have the power to incite the need for revenge in some hearts. When Mary's mother died, I promised to take the child in and raise her under another name. And I will keep her secret until such time as no more danger exists. For instance, if she were to marry, well, then it would be up to her husband to take on the secret and protect her with his name. Am I getting through to you, son? Lift up your chin from your chest and show me I am not wrong in my estimation of your feelings."

CHAPTER TWELVE

Kitty was in the small, sunny morning room, engrossed in one of her favorite occupations—embroidering. Since joining the Ruffton household, she had decorated endless scarves, aprons, slippers, caps and stockings for all and sundry, much to the delight of the servants to whom she presented them as gifts, and to the dismay of the rest of the household, who were still trying to figure out how to dispose of the stuff without hurting the dear child's feelings.

At the moment she had just finished putting the final touches to a pair of garters meant for her beloved Dexter. She held one of the garters up to read once more the inscription she had fashioned with dainty stitches: "Pray keep me tight from morn till night." Smiling serenely, she then cradled the thing to her bosom, knowing Dexter would be overjoyed with her surprise.

"Daydreaming again, sister mine?" spoke a voice from the doorway, and Kitty whirled in her seat to see her brother Jerome lounging against the doorjamb, his hands in his pockets.

"Oh, Gemini, Jerry, you gave me such a fright! How did you get past Perkins?"

Jerome dismissed the thought of Ruffton's imposing butler with a toss of his blond head. "He knows I'm family. What did you think he'd do, bar the door?"

Kitty quickly lowered her eyes, remembering how she had heard Sir Henry grumble after Jerry's last visit. "Let that sort in once and he might take it upon himself to make a habit of it," he had told Rachel, winking broadly to Kitty to soften his words.

Sauntering over to a nearby chair, Toland dropped his lean body into it and demanded Kitty ring for refreshments. This so flustered the girl, who began saying something about being a guest in the house herself, that Jerome finally cut her off by the simple means of giving voice to a particularly vulgar expression.

Once he was sure he had her attention, he leaned forward in his seat and told her in a low voice filled with malice, "You ignorant chit! I've set you up so that you travel in the first circles, knee-deep in London swells, and what do you do? You persist in defacing innocent garments with your ridiculous stitchery and cowering like some half-wit scullery maid when asked to behave in line with your station. Even worse, instead of peacocking about in society like any sensible girl, you go and tumble into love with some penniless loose screw who doesn't know his hat from his hindquarters."

And Kitty *was* cowering, right up until the moment her brother had the nerve—the awful temerity—to insult her beloved Dexter. Then the little kitten reacted like a lioness whose cub was in peril. "You shameless creature!" she exclaimed in her high, childish voice. "You run through Papa's inheritance, let our estate go under the hammer, and then try to marry me off to some rich man who will pay for your reckless way of living. And if that isn't bad enough, you have set me up—as you call it—with no less than three families, just to gain entrance to their houses to rob them. Jerry," she intoned indignantly, "you are a horrid, ghastly man!"

Jerome hoisted himself slowly to his feet and rewarded his sister's outburst with a languid clapping of his hands. "I'd throttle you for that, sister mine, except that I've other fish to fry right now, thanks to your information about Miss Mary Lawrence's nocturnal habits. And this time I'll earn enough to keep me plump in the pocket for a long, long time to come. Resign yourself to the fact that I won't be carting you about any longer. If I don't see you again—good-bye, dearest Catherine. May you rot in hell!"

He had made it halfway to the door before Kitty could find her voice. "Does this mean you will give your permission for Dexter and me to marry? After all, what difference can it make to you?"

Jerome wheeled about slowly, a nasty smile on his face. "Oh, didn't I tell you? How remiss of me. Your swain dropped by this morning, brimful of April and May. I had to deny his request for your hand, seeing as how he refused to see the need to reimburse me for raising you. I could have left you to the workhouse when our dear Papa kicked off, couldn't I, though Rutherford didn't see it my way. It was something I most particularly regret, but I had no other choice than to decline his offer to remove you from my responsibility. I am your guardian until you reach your majority. Let's see —that's a little less than five years, isn't it? Surely not too long to wait for *true love*, is it?"

"Oh, Jerry, you're never going to destroy my happiness like this, are you?" Kitty pleaded, dropping out of her chair to fall to her knees, the pleading supplicant.

His answer was a blood-chilling laugh, and then

silence. Somehow she dragged herself to her feet and made her way to her chamber before collapsing on the bed in a torrent of tears.

And in her despondency, she forgot all about Jerome's hints as to a plot concerning Mary.

Sir Henry's library doubled as his private office. It was not often that he allowed anyone save Perkins inside it, and the butler was only exempt because even such important surroundings did need occasional dusting to remain habitable.

But now Rachel was sitting poised for battle in one of the oversized leather wingback chairs, obviously very much agitated. She had dared to enter the library without permission, believing herself to be acting within the rights of a person who had been appointed as chaperon to a young, volatile girl. "I say to you again, Henry, I don't think I can continue bear-leading your ward. I saw her tippy-toeing into her chambers last night past one o'clock, clad in the most outrageous costume it has ever been my misfortune to view. Lucy took the last of my fight from me. It's time I realized that I am past the age when I can be safely relied upon to keep a strong-willed young miss on a stout enough leash. Henry! Have you been listening to a single word I've been saying?"

Sir Henry, who had been sitting behind his desk, his fingertips steepled in front of his nose, lowered his hands to let his smile show. "Of course I've been listening. I've always listened to you."

"No you haven't," came Rachel's sharp rejoinder, for she was feeling quite put upon this morning. "If you had, I never would have allowed Reggie Moore to—never mind. That's all ancient history anyway. What's more to the point—*what* are you going to do about Mary? Don't you think it's time you told her the truth before she does something that lands us all in the suds?"

Sir Henry rose to walk round the desk and lean a hip against one of its corners. "*Cant*, Rachel? Since when have you descended into slang? Perhaps you're right. All those years spent with the younger generation have corrupted you."

"Don't try to fob me off with that sad attempt at wit, Henry; I've known you too long for that. Now, since your lack of surprise tells me that you already know about Mary's actions of last night, perhaps you will allow me into the secret."

Smiling one of his most cherubic smiles, Ruffton announced: "My ward's in love with your nephew."

Rachel sat back in her chair and sniffed. "Tell me something I don't already know, if you please."

Sir Henry went on undaunted. "Your nephew is besotted to the point of idiocy with my ward."

Raising a hand to her lips, Rachel gave an exaggerated yawn. "And with this love he has also acquired an attic positively crawling with maggots. Yes, dear, I know. Again I have lapsed sadly into cant. But you begin to bore me, sir. Get on with it."

So goaded, Sir Henry went on to describe his late-night meeting with Rule, right down to the part where Tristan had refused Sir Henry's offer of an explanation of Mary's past, preferring first to win the heart of his fair lady and then hearing the full details of the story from her own lips.

"But she doesn't *know* the full story," Rachel was forced to point out. "Lord, I shudder to think of Tristan's reaction once he learns who Mary's father was!"

"Precisely, my dear," Sir Henry replied. "Which is exactly why I am allowing the boy to be noble about the thing. Once they've explored their love for each other a little bit, the truth should lose some of its sting. You know Tristan, Rachel. This isn't going to be easy for him."

Rachel shook her head. "You were always the master of understatement, Henry."

But Ruffton wasn't really listening anymore. Rachel's slip of the tongue about Reggie Moore, the twelfth Lord Hetherington, had sent his mind winging back into the past. What on earth did that oily womanizer have to do with anything? Mary had hinted to him that it was time he and Rachel had a talk about the breakup of their engagement —something about the two of them resolving an old misunderstanding—but for the life of him Henry couldn't remember Reggie being a part of it.

"Rachel," he said now, taking one of her hands in his, "tell me about Hetherington. You said I didn't listen to you when you wanted to talk about him. I'm listening now."

Rachel stiffened, trying in vain to draw back her hand. "Why should I tell you? It's more than you deserve, when you know as well as I you found me guilty at the time without even pretending you wished to hear my side of the story."

Ruffton gave her hand a squeeze. "I am an old man now, but my memories of that time have always seemed clear enough to me. Why can't I remember Moore figuring in them? Satisfy me in this, my dear. I think we might both learn something from the exercise."

He sounded so sincere, thought Rachel. But it was all so embarrassing. Look at him, sitting there so patiently, waiting. And there *was* Mary's odd suggestion—something about misunderstandings between them. Maybe . . .

Rachel gave a deep sigh, then capitulated. "You know how tiresomely volatile I was in my youth," she began hesitantly. "Perhaps that's why I have been able to deal so well with my various charges. Well, you were so busy doing something with the government that you paid less and less attention to me during those last weeks before our wedding was to take place."

"I know," Sir Henry broke in to confess. "I wanted to be sure no emergencies would crop up to keep us from our wedding trip. I had planned a leisurely tour of the Lake District. I thought you would have liked that."

Grimacing, Rachel quipped, "Well, thank you for that, Henry. You have surpassed my expectations and succeeded in making me feel even lower than ever about what I did. If I may continue?" she asked, tilting her head as she waited for his signal to go on.

"I promise not to interrupt again, my dear," he told her, lifting her hand to place a kiss on her wrist.

Flustered, Rachel cleared her throat and began again. "Anyway, Reggie was always hanging about my skirts, declaring his undying love, so I thought . . . maybe . . . maybe going into the garden with Reggie would shake you into showing me some attention. Well, how was I to know that busybody Harriet Whitstone would go running hotfoot to you with some harebrained story about my . . . my gown being undone? And who would have thought you'd send round that simply horrid, stiff note saying you would allow me to be the one to cry off . . . and then lope off like that to the country without even so much as talking to me again. Oh, drat it all anyway, Henry, what does it matter now? Give me your handkerchief, I'm blubbering like a schoolgirl."

"But—but," Henry stammered momentarily as he tried to marshal his thoughts. "I can't believe this! I never heard anything about you and Moore. It was Harriet who tricked *me* into being alone with her at Lord Malmsley's rout and then ran to tell her mother I had all but raped her behind the shrubbery," Henry said, confusion evident in his voice. "I *had* to cry off our engagement, seeing as how Harriet's father had a pistol—at least figuratively—to my head. It was either that or involve you in scandal."

He stopped speaking for a moment, as if considering what Rachel had said. "Reggie Moore, eh. Never did like that rum fellow above half. Lucky for him he's married to that Isobel creature now, else I'd have his liver and lights. Isobel's more than enough punishment, no matter how well to go her father was. Lord, has a face that would turn the cream, doesn't she?"

Rachel closed her eyes tightly and shook her head. Why was Henry prosing on about ugly Isobel? Didn't he realize what the two of them had just learned? It had all been a crazy mistake—each thinking himself the reason for their broken engagement. Why, if it weren't for Harriet Whitstone, she and Henry would have been wed twenty years ago. Kill Reggie? Hang Reggie! It was *Harriet's* blood Rachel wanted!

"Harriet died last year, did you know?" Henry was saying now. "She ran away with her dancing master before her father could get me to the altar, thank the Lord, and spent her last years in some benighted Irish village hiding from her husband's creditors."

The two onetime lovers remained silent for some minutes, Sir Henry still keeping hold of Rachel's hand, each deep in his own thoughts. In the background they could hear the low rumble of male voices and then Mary's rather overdone welcome of Lord Rule as a morning caller. From the sounds emanating from the hallway, it was easy to figure out that Tristan had called to ask Mary out for a drive and that Mary was agreeable to the plan. A few moments later the heavy front door closed and the house was quiet once more.

Henry allowed the silence to stretch nearly to the snapping point before saying softly, "We're a pretty pair of fools, d'you know that? We let it slip away from us, didn't we? Our love. Our youth. But it's not too late for a bit of connubial happiness, is it, my love?"

Rachel lifted her tear-drenched eyes to gaze at his dear, cherubic face. "Connubial happiness?" she repeated, giving him a watery smile. "Why, Henry, are you talking smutty?"

"More cant?" he observed, shaking his head and trying to hide the moistness in his own eyes. Slowly, he drew Rachel to her feet as he too stood. "Say whatever you like, my dearest. Us old fogies have the right to be as smutty or as syrupy as we please." He stopped speaking for a moment, then went on, his voice a bit husky, "There's never been anyone but you, Rachel. You know that, don't you?"

"Or for me, Henry," Rachel returned on a sigh. "We'll scandalize everyone, you know. Why, we've even been living under the same roof."

Henry was pulling her closer. "Ah, yes, but we have had Mary here as chaperon."

Rachel lifted her head from the resting place it had found against Henry's ample chest. "Mary as chaperon? *That* will certainly cause a royal tow-row!"

"And again cant?" Sir Henry observed, his head lowering toward hers. "I must make it my first duty to find a way to end this deplorable new habit of yours, my dear."

Lifting her face to meet him halfway, Rachel

whispered, "You were ever a master at tactical maneuver, my dearest Henry," before allowing herself to be silenced by his warm mouth.

Dexter and Kitty were alone in the second drawing room, seeing that Mary was out driving with Tristan, and Rachel, whose job it was to act as chaperon at times like these, was still in the library, comporting herself in a most unchaperon-like way.

The two young people were holding hands and sighing deep sighs that were enough to melt the coldest heart.

"I approached your brother this morning to—"

Kitty sighed. "I know. 'Tis monstrous cruel of him—"

"He's been running shy of luck at the gaming houses of late. Probably hanging out for a suitor more plump in the pocket—"

"Jerry has always been horridly disobliging—"

"A cod."

"Oh, Dexter!"

"Oh, Kitty!"

There was more handholding and more sighing before Dexter spoke again. "He didn't even want to hear about Great-Aunt Felicity. I'm her heir, you know, and she ain't well, not that I wish her below ground, you understand. We'd be well enough to go for now, but I couldn't spare any for your brother."

"He once took me to Bagnigge Wells and called it a holiday," Kitty mused aloud. "You're right, dearest. Jerry's a *cod*."

"I just left then, like some crack-brained cringe in the boots. Julian would have popped him one, I know it. I guess I still held out some hope we could bring him round. But now you say he's told you no too." He gave out yet another deep sigh. "I should have popped him."

"Bagnigge Wells is frequented by only the lowest sort of tradesmen. And the sheets were damp. Why should I be loyal to someone who lets me catch my death on damp sheets?"

"I should have just stood my ground and *told* him we were going to be married. That's what I should have done. *No!* I should have just turned my back on him and his refusal and carried you off to Gretna."

"Gretna? Gretna Green?" Clearly some of Dexter's ramblings had gotten through.

Dexter could feel his knees beginning to knock together and he swallowed down hard on a gulp. "Yes, Gretna!" he repeated with some bravado. "I can see no other way, for I will not be forced to wait until you no longer need your guardian's permission. Are you game?"

As a proposal it lacked something in the way of romance, but Kitty didn't seem to notice. After blinking her wide blue eyes a time or two, she returned a rather incoherent answer that Dexter decided to take for a yes, then burst into tears.

"That's my girl!" the young Lothario exclaimed bracingly. "Oh, what a rare to-do this will cause. Come on, Kitty, buck up, do. Can't have you acting the watering pot all the way to Scotland. Damp enough there as it is."

Kitty did her best to quell the tumult in her heart, for tears had always sent her nose to running in a most unappealing way. "Oh, Gemini, Dex, do you really think—"

Dexter silenced her doubts with a kiss—a kiss that left them so spent that after it was over they both sighed yet again and fell back against the settee to look wonderingly up at the ceiling.

"Oh, Gemini," they breathed in unison.

CHAPTER THIRTEEN

It wasn't exactly the most beautiful day for a ride in the country, but Mary didn't notice. She was still quite full of herself over the success of her exploits of the previous evening, especially after her late-night vigil had been rewarded at last by the sight of one very-much-on-his-dignity Lord Tristan Rule stomping down the flagway, Sir Henry waving him on his way.

"My trick, sir, I fancy," she had whispered from her position hidden behind the window drapery. Although sleep had been a long time in coming— for she could not, now that the deed was done, figure out whether it pleased her or distressed her to have played Rule like some monkey on a string —she had decided in the end to simply rejoice in her success and await further developments.

That it had turned out to be a short wait only delighted her the more. Rule had shown himself at Sir Henry's at an almost indecently early hour, begging her to accompany him for a ride in his curricle. She had been so full of herself she had even dared to tease him as they passed by London Bridge that it was lucky for her it was no longer the custom to impale the heads of traitors on spikes at either end of the drawbridge gate—a tongue-in-cheek reference to his earlier suspicions of her that had Rule grumbling into his cravat for the next few miles.

It was this headiness with her success that led them to their first real conversation, as Tristan had been extremely closemouthed ever since he had handed her up into the curricle. "Did you enjoy yourself last evening, my lord?" she teased.

"I bloody well did not!" Tristan responded hotly, looking at her piercingly.

Struggling not to smile, Mary schooled her features into an expression of injured innocence. "Oh dear, forgive me for asking. I had the headache and had to retire early, but the gathering seemed to be lively enough. Perhaps you had a bad turn at the tables?"

Tristan's face darkened as he realized she had purposely drawn him into disclosing his reaction to her nocturnal excursion without ever revealing her guilt. "Now *that* ties it!" he exploded, pulling the horses off the road, driving them through a sparse wood and deep into a grassy field.

Without another word he sprang down from the seat and set the brake before going round to haul Mary down almost roughly. Taking her unwilling hand in his, he growled, "Let's walk."

"Why not?" Mary chirped sarcastically. "I never liked these slippers above half anyway. Don't you go worrying your head about the damp grass, sir, for I shall not let it weigh with me."

Tristan stopped abruptly and turned to look at her. A lingering glance from those dark eyes she wouldn't have minded, but this was an outright stare, raking her from head to toe. By the time he was done, she felt she had been stripped down to her shift and had to fight not to raise her hands and cover herself.

"I followed you last night," he said at last, in a voice that chilled her to her very marrow.

Mary could feel her knees beginning to turn to jelly, and this immediately made her angry. "So?" she asked, lifting her chin, trying to give him back whatever he was able to dish out—doubled! "I was only being agreeable." She shrugged her shoulders. "You wanted intrigue. I was only giving you what you desired."

A small tic began to work in Rule's cheek. "And I'm sure you enjoyed yourself quite royally at my expense," he admitted before roaring, "but did it ever occur to you that you could have gotten yourself killed—or worse—walking about London unescorted at that time of night?"

Mary reached up to untie the ribbons on her bonnet, baring her gleaming hair to the watery sun. "Don't be ridiculous. You were there, weren't you? You wouldn't have let anything happen to me."

"Don't bet on it," Rule returned coldly.

Letting her bonnet hang upside down from its ribbons, Mary began walking about, picking wildflowers and using her headgear as a basket. "I hedged my bets, as I've heard it said. I had Jennie's grooms, Tiny and Goliath, along as well. I was never in any real danger. I'm not a complete idiot."

"No! Only a partial idiot!" Rule shot back at her before the entirety of what she had said sunk into his hot head. He reached out a hand and grabbed hold of her elbow. "Tiny and Goliath? They were there at *my* instigation. Kit lent them to *me*!"

They stood there, staring at each other in disbelief for several moments, before the absurdity of the thing finally began to dawn on them. Jennie and Kit—and most probably Lucy and Julian as well—had been having themselves a fine old time at their expense. Why, they were probably laughing themselves sick at this very moment, thinking they had pulled off a major joke.

The dimple appeared in Mary's left cheek just as

Rule's shoulders began to shake. "What a fine pair of fools we are!" Mary chortled, dropping to her knees on the grass. "Taken in like greenhorns by a foursome of matchmakers. Wait till I see Lucy. Oh, she'll be crowing about this for a fortnight!"

"Don't forget Julian," Rule said, falling down beside her to lean back on his elbows. "He must be full of himself after turning the tables on his wife. Whoever said he was stuffy? I wonder if it occurred to him that we might both require the servants on the same night?"

"Can you doubt it?" Mary asked, giggling. "I wondered why Tiny was so obliging when I asked for his services. He said, 'I be goin' there anyways,' when I asked him to accompany me to Green Park. I wondered about it at the time, but I just assumed I hadn't understood him correctly. Oh lordy, what do you suppose they think of us?"

"I'd rather not guess, thank you anyway," Tristan said, yet another laugh escaping him.

Now that Rule seemed to be in a better mood, Mary began to feel a bit guilty about the poem. After all, it must have been quite embarrassing to have Sir Henry read what she had written. Picking up a handful of the flowers she had gathered, she leaned forward and began dropping them one by one onto Tristan's chest. "You really aren't obtuse, you know. It just fit the poem."

Rule let his body recline fully on the ground so that he could use his hand to take hold of Mary's wrist. "And I suppose you only employed the word *ass* because it rhymed so well with *class*?"

Mary used her free hand to pick up a blossom and tickle Rule's nose with it. "W-e-l-l, *actually—*" she began before Rule, moving so quickly she was unable to defend herself, had grabbed hold of both her wrists and reversed their positions, with her now lying on the ground, staring up at him as he hovered menacingly over her body.

Time hung suspended for long moments as she admired his handsome face, from his squared chin to his chiseled brow. The laughter was gone from his dark eyes, but it wasn't anger that she saw in them now. Oh, she thought to herself inanely, if Rachel could see her nephew's eyes right now, she'd have me locked in my room for the remainder of the Season. What was she thinking? If Rachel could see them now, in this oh, so compromising position, she would have Sir Henry posting the banns before the sun set!

"Tris—Tristan?" she breathed at last. "I apologize for everything I've done. It was silly of me to do it; I can't imagine what maggot I'd let into my head to think to tease you in the first place. You really should let me up now. Tristan?"

"Not until you've told me why you felt it necessary to hoax me in the first place," he returned, freeing one of her wrists so that he could brush back a curl that had strayed across her cheek. "I had already admitted you were not the spy I first thought you. Why did you persist in setting yourself up as guilty? I hate to admit it, but you gave me a few bad turns when I thought you were up to some mischief."

Mary, used to being the object of schemes designed by some young gentleman to pique *her* interest, was loath to admit she had planned the entire project in order to keep Tristan interested in her—and away from his estates in the country. But that strange "something" she saw in his eyes, that look that was rapidly turning her insides to soft pudding, had her tossing her pride to the winds. "Having a secret seemed the only way to keep you in town," she admitted in a whisper, turning her face away from his gaze.

Oh Lord, she felt ready to sink. What if he laughed at her? What if he teased her now about *her* infatuation with him, as she had done him at the theater? What if he got to his feet and just walked away, having lost interest now that he knew there was no reason for him to be concerned about some dark secret in her past?

Just when Mary thought she was going to either faint or explode, Tristan shifted his body slightly to lie belly down in the grass beside her, turning her face to his by placing a finger under her chin. "It worked, you know," he informed her gently. "You have succeeded in riveting my attention. And much as I hate to admit that Lucy and Jennie could ever be right in anything, I can only tell you that it doesn't matter a fig whether you've got a secret in your past or not—I am top over tail in love with you, Mary Lawrence."

"Oh, Tristan," Mary breathed, a tremulous smile on her lips, her green eyes bright with unshed tears. "Do you think there was ever such a muddled courting? I love you too!"

All thoughts of secrets, schemes, or threats of blackmail scattered to the four winds as Tristan used his finger to guide Mary's chin even closer to him. Turning slightly so that their bodies lay together in the grass, he leaned forward and moved his lips against hers in a soft, exploratory kiss.

Their arms moved to twine around each other, causing their bodies to be pressed close from neck to hip, a movement that unleashed their volatile emotions until they were clinging to each other desperately, their mouths fused together passionately, melting and reforming in the heat of their desire.

For so many years Rule had taken his pleasures where he found them, more to assuage his physical needs rather than to satisfy anything within his soul. This was different, so wondrously different; holding Mary in his arms had set loose tender feelings he didn't believe he possessed.

Along with the burning need he had to hold her, touch her, possess her, to claim her now and forever as his and his alone, there was an awareness of her fragility, her innocence, her blind trust in him never to hurt her. He could feel her trembling within his embrace, awakening to the needs of her body, and, while frightened of her intense reaction, willing to place herself entirely in his power.

Slowly, and with patently obvious regret, Tristan eased Mary's arms from about his neck and, with a few nibbling kisses, ended their embrace. "Since you have said you do not believe me to be obtuse, my love, I will return the compliment by telling you that I believe you to be intelligent enough to know, as I do, that we are in danger of crossing a line that should remain uncrossed until after our wedding."

Mary ducked her head against his broad chest to hide her flaming cheeks. "Is—is it always like this?" she mumbled into his cravat, trying hard to control her breathing.

She could hear the rumble of his laughter through the cloth of his shirt. "No, my sweetings, it is even better—much better. But now that I have a secret from you, I believe it best if I withhold it until our wedding night." He leaned back a little to look down at the top of her head. "You will marry me, Miss Mary Lawrence, won't you?"

She rolled away from him and hopped gingerly to her feet, brushing a few twigs and leaves from her skirts. "I'd better say yes, Tris, now that I will be returning to my uncle and your so-astute aunt with grass stains on my back."

Mary pressed her fingers to her mouth, giggling as Rule produced an exaggerated look of shock on his face. "Oh dear, that sounded horribly *fast*, didn't it? But if we are to be wed, I believe it is time you learned that my real name is not Mary

Lawrence. You were right about that at least, you nosy devil you."

Rule made a small ceremony out of rising to his feet and brushing down his clothes. He had been so caught up in their mutual passion, so relieved to finally understand his reason for being so intrigued with Mary from the moment he had first clapped eyes on her, so heady with the knowledge that Mary was at last his, that any secrets in her past were, quite frankly, the very last thing on his mind.

He reached over to draw a small twig slowly from Mary's tangled curls. "Sir Henry told me your parents left you in his care when they died. He also told me that they had some enemies of some sort who might have taken it into their heads to revenge themselves on you if he were to let your true identity become common knowledge. He also said," Tristan went on, bending to retrieve her bonnet and taking her hand as they began their walk back to the curricle, "that he would tell me everything I wanted to know if I really wanted to hear it."

"And did you?" Mary asked, leaning into him as they walked along. "What am I saying? Of course you did. I can't imagine you turning down such a grand opportunity."

"I did not," he corrected, tweaking her nose. "I stopped him, telling him I would learn the rest of your secret from you. Not that I can for the life of me understand why it should matter a snap now, or why it *ever* seemed to matter."

"That's what I've been telling Sir Henry, until I'm blue in the face. He's had me buried deep in Sussex ever since I was eight, surrounding me with servants that I know full well were hired with my protection in mind. And all because my father was French! How silly—half the *ton* could claim French blood."

"Sir Henry was ever a cautious sort," Tristan told her as he made to help her up onto the curricle seat. "I'm sure he had his reasons at the time."

"If you say so, Tris," Mary relented, standing on tiptoe to kiss his cheek before moving to climb up into the curricle. "But I believe I would like to use my real name for the marriage ceremony, even if I have been known as Mary Lawrence for so long that I probably won't answer to it when someone calls to me. Marie Lisette Vivienne St. Laurent—it has a certain ring to it, don't you think? Tristan . . . Tristan? You're breaking my fingers! What's wrong?"

"St. Laurent?" he asked in a strangled voice. "*Jules* St. Laurent?"

"Yes, have you heard of him? Uncle Henry says he was quite well known. Tristan, whatever is the matter with you?" Mary had gained the seat by now, and she wheeled about to watch Rule as he walked around the curricle to the other side, his face as dark as a thundercloud. "My father escaped the Terror and fled to England, where he met my mother. Uncle Henry says the people who confiscated the family estates may have thought I presented a danger to them, especially now that the war is over. As if I wanted anything to do with some moldy acres in Grenoble."

Mary knew she was babbling, but Tristan was scaring her so, she didn't know what else to do. "Uncle Henry was telling me the truth, wasn't he?" she almost begged. "Tristan, for God's sake, *speak* to me! Say *something*!"

"I've kept you out too long," he said at last, his voice wooden. "My aunt will tear a strip off my hide if I don't return her chick to her soon."

"A pox on propriety!" Mary snapped, her fears overriding every other emotion save the love she had for this man who now seemed so distant, so unapproachable. "What do you know about my father that I don't?"

Rule turned to her slowly, all emotion drained from his eyes and voice. "You'd better let Sir Henry explain, as it's been his secret for so long. I only wish to God it still was."

"But—but—" Mary began, then lapsed into silence. If she knew nothing else, she knew that Rule wouldn't be budged from his position. She could only cudgel her own brain as they rode along in silence.

Was her happiness to be so short-lived? Would Tristan—now that he knew all there was to know about her, and, obviously, more than even *she* knew—retract his proposal?

She couldn't stand not knowing. Crossing all her fingers in her lap, she took a deep breath and asked desperately, "Does this mean you no longer wish us to be married?"

In that same dead voice she had quickly learned to dread, Rule replied, "I said I'd marry you, and I'm not known for going back on my word."

Stung, Mary retorted smartly, "Well, don't let that bother you, I'll not blab it about that the great Tristan Rule went back on his word."

"*I love you, damn it!*" Tristan shouted at her, making her jump. "You just have to give me some time. I just have to have some time alone—to think."

Mary bit down hard on her bottom lip and the taste of her own blood filled her mouth. "You do that, Tristan," she answered softly. "And so will I."

Just as the curricle was passing London Bridge, the skies opened up and it began to rain. Mary silently blessed the raindrops, for they hid her falling tears.

CHAPTER FOURTEEN

The door to the library slammed shut with enough force to rattle the candlesticks on the mantelpiece across the room. Sir Henry looked up from the dispatch he was reading just in time to see his ward turn the lock and then remove the key, stuffing it into the bodice of her gown.

The girl looked a sorry enough shrimp, her gown and pelisse darkened with rainwater, her straw bonnet limp and drooping down over her eyes. "Is nothing sacred anymore?" he asked with a smile, releasing the dispatch and leaning back comfortably in his oversized leather chair. "First Rachel, although the results were well worth the upheaval, and now you, Mary. I may be overreacting, but somehow I don't believe yours to be a social 'break in.' Perhaps it is time to have a talk with Perkins; I believe, that as a bodyguard at least, the man might at last be getting past it."

The only answer to his words was Mary's short, unladylike exclamation as she struggled exasperatedly to untie the tangled wet ribbons of her bonnet and toss the offending headgear into a corner.

"In case you're wondering about the results of Rachel's visit to my sanctum," Sir Henry went on placidly, rising to walk around the desk and pour the two balloon glasses of brandy he privately felt to be in order, "I am happy to tell you that we have resolved all our mistaken conclusions of the past and are now betrothed once more. Rachel was quite a belle in her day, you know, and could still give many a run for their money. To have captured her affections, not once, but twice, has me standing before you feeling rather full of myself, I don't mind telling you."

"My felicitations, Uncle," Mary said sarcastically, flinging herself into the chair Rachel had occupied earlier. "As it seems to take you several decades to resolve personal problems, may I then look ahead to, say, 1840, in the hope you will have by that time figured a way out of the 'mistaken conclusion' now destroying *my* life?"

"You and Tristan have had a misunderstanding?" Ruffton prompted, handing Mary one of the glasses.

"Need you ask?" Mary replied dampeningly before saluting her uncle and then taking a healthy sip of the brandy. The unaccustomed strong spirit hit the back of her throat like liquid fire, and it was only after several minutes spent thumping his ward between the shoulder blades as she coughed and choked that Sir Henry could hope to hear exactly what had transpired.

"Stop trying to cosset me!" Mary told him indignantly, jerking her body away from Sir Henry's ministering hand once she recovered her voice. "And don't try to hoax me either. It's time and more I find out exactly who I am, for I am certainly not who you say I am. Start with my father, if you please, for it would seem the name St. Laurent is at the heart of the problem."

Sir Henry returned to his chair behind the desk and stared at his ward over the steeple of his pressed-together fingertips. Obviously the child had told Rule her true name and the results had been even worse than he had feared. "Did Lord Rule cast aspersions on your father, my dear?"

"N-no," Mary admitted, searching in her reticule for her handkerchief. "He . . . he . . . Oh, Uncle Henry," she imparted shakily, "he asked me to marry him!" She then proceeded to hiccup before bursting into loud sobs.

Sir Henry tilted his head and nodded once. "Marry you, eh? I did give him my blessings last night, so that doesn't surprise me overmuch, knowing Tristan's penchant for rushing his fences. But really, my pet, if you don't want him, all you have to do is say so. There's no need to resort to tears."

Mary scrubbed at her damp cheeks before looking at her guardian as if he had suddenly grown another nose. "Not want him? Oh, Uncle Henry, how could you possibly be so obtuse? Of course I *want* him! I love him!"

Ruffton sat front on his chair, pointing a finger at Mary's outthrust chin. "It would take an absolute idiot not to see that you're overset, but I do believe I've taken enough sauce from you, child. I am not so obtuse as to be unable to connect your tears with your demand to know more about your father. You told Tristan your real name, didn't you? Furthermore, I believe I can take it from your histrionic outburst—breaking into my library and then hiding the key in your bodice like some character in a melodrama—that his reaction to your disclosure wasn't all you had hoped it would be. He didn't . . . er . . . *hurt* you in any way, did he?"

Mary bit her lip and shook her head in the negative. "Forgive me for being so rude, Uncle. I admit to being a bit hysterical. And no, Tris didn't hurt me. At least not so you can see," she responded shakily, slowly getting herself back under control.

"Everything was perfectly lovely, actually, until I told him I wished to be married using my real name. And then . . . and then . . ."

"And then he began ranting and raving and slamming his fist into his hand and generally making a cake of himself?" Ruffton offered, knowing his man well.

Mary shook her head. "If only he had. That I would have understood. He's so adorable when he's in one of his rages—like a small boy throwing a tantrum. I could have handled that. Instead, he just suddenly lost all the color in his face and refused to so much as peek in my direction all the way home.

"Oh, he did speak to me once, to tell me again that he loved me—he *shouted* it, actually—but I can't say as I was much comforted by his declaration." She looked at her uncle beseechingly. "He's not acting true to form, Uncle, that's what really worries me. Whatever he knows about my father, it must be serious indeed, to have him turning from lover into stranger within the blinking of an eye."

"You landed him a real settler this time, pet, that's for certain," Sir Henry agreed gloomily. "But give him time," he ended by way of sympathy. "He'll recover—if his love for you is as deep as both Rachel and I believe it to be."

"He's leaving late today for his estate in Surrey," Mary supplied dully. "To 'think.' He told me that as he escorted me to the door. Then he left me standing on the doorstep and sprang his horses away as if the hounds of Hell were after him."

Henry nodded several times, considering this development. "Good, good. Tris has an ugly temper; it's a good thing he took himself off. He has to work through this thing alone. I wish I could have spared you this, Mary, my dear, spared the both of you, but it is better to start your married life with no secrets between you."

"We have one now, Uncle," Mary quipped with a hint of her old spirit. "*He* knows who I am—and *I* don't. Perhaps you will at last deem it appropriate in your master plan to enlighten me so that I can at least understand why Tristan is so upset."

Sir Henry was barely attending, as he was lost deep in his own thoughts. "I should have never told you your real name. You had forgotten it, along with everything else, after the shock of it all. But how was I to know you would go tumbling into love with a man like Tristan, a man so strict in his loyalties? Perhaps I shall call Rachel in here; she'll know how best to go on."

"Forgotten it all? What have I forgotten? And how? And what do Tristan's rigid loyalties have to do with it? Uncle!" Mary demanded loudly, breaking into Sir Henry's reverie. "What on earth are you talking about?"

Ruffton looked at his ward, seeing her as she was ten years earlier, her clothing burned and smoky from the fire, her auburn hair singed nearly to the roots on one side of her head, but her chin still held high like the little aristocrat that she was.

He sighed deeply, giving up the memory of the child who had so tugged at his heart and looked intently at the young woman who sat before him now, damp, bedraggled, but still every inch the aristocrat. "You'd prefer the unvarnished truth, I imagine?" he asked resignedly.

"Infinitely," she agreed, raising her chin yet another degree.

The heavy velvet draperies were closed tight against the late-afternoon sun, throwing the large chamber into near darkness. Rachel tiptoed into the room until she could see the outline of Mary's huddled body as it lay atop the high tester bed, facing the wall.

All in all it's been quite a day for the poor infant, the older woman thought as she crossed the carpet silently to sit down on the edge of the bed, agreeable to waiting in silence until Mary chose to acknowledge her presence.

It didn't take long. "Go way," Mary mumbled into her pillow, making backward shooing motions with her left hand. "I'm not receiving at the moment. Come back later."

"When?" Rachel nudged, her heart going out to Mary.

"Late September—I just might be willing to talk then," came the answer before the pillow was lifted and repositioned directly over Mary's head. "Now go *away!*"

"You plan going into a genteel decline, child? How crushingly ordinary. Really, I had come to expect better from you."

Rachel's last statement had Mary flinging the pillow away from her as she shot into a sitting position to glare at her chaperon and accuse: "You knew, didn't you? You knew all along! How could you let me go out in society when you knew? Why give me a taste of what could have been, when you realized perfectly well that society would shun me if they knew the truth? Oh lord, I may as well set on my caps now, for once the story gets out and the world is done with my good name, I'll be as welcome as the plague in the fashionable drawing rooms, and you know it."

"Oh, I see," Rachel said placidly. "And that's what matters to you, does it? What society will think?"

"No. I don't care a snap what society thinks, and well you know that too," Mary said softly, yet

another bout of tears not far from the surface.
"It's Tris. If he pilloried me before, when he
had only his suspicions for fuel, he'll hate me
now. You didn't see his face, Rachel. He could
barely stand to look at me. And I don't blame
him."

"I imagine you're refining too much on that 'sins
of the father being visited on the children' thing.
Tristan is shocked, of course he is, but it's you he's
asked to marry, not your father." Rachel reached
over to wipe Mary's tears with her own handkerchief. "Give him a little time, my dear, he'll come
around. He'll go off to Surrey in one of his mad
takings like a sulky little boy for a bit, but he loves
you, and in the end he'll see that your father's
actions have nothing to do with you. Trust me in
this, for I know Tristan well."

Mary took possession of the handkerchief and
blew her nose. "I still can't take it all in. I just
thought no one had much memory of anything
below the age of eight. It never occurred to me
that I was any different."

"Sir Henry saw no reason to try to prod your
memory, since it could only cause you pain,"
Rachel explained now. "It was your mother's
dying wish that Henry take care of you and he did
the best he knew how, installing you in Sussex
with his trusted retired soldiers to keep you safe.
Why, your memory was so thoroughly erased that
you spoke both English and French interchange-
ably, not really knowing which was correct. Henry
had you surrounded by only English-speaking
servants until you were fourteen, to help you
forget. It was only then that he employed your
French tutor, who Henry tells me considered you
to be quite a prodigy in languages, as you picked
up his lessons so well."

"My mother was English?" Mary prompted, as
she had not asked Sir Henry very much about her

mother—the story of her father had consumed her too much for that.

Rachel nodded. "I never met her, although we were much of the same age and social station. She was the daughter of a second son, none too plump in the pocket, so she was never presented. But it is from her that you got your beauty, Sir Henry tells me, and your good heart."

"You don't have to tell me from whom I inherited my less desirable traits," Mary quipped halfheartedly. "No wonder I was so ready to indulge in intrigue with Tristan. It was bred in the bone."

Sir Henry had already told Mary the truth about her father, so there was no reason for Rachel to try to dress the thing up in fine linen now. "Your father, aristocratic French blood to the side, was a villain of the first water, Mary. His main interest in life was the acquisition of money, and he made it by selling secrets to both France and England at the same time. That dual betrayal of trust cost many lives on both sides, and in the end St. Laurent forfeited his own life for his crimes. It was very much in character for him to start his house on fire to try to cover his escape that last time, not caring a single bit that his wife and child stood to perish in the blaze."

Her chin resting on her chest, Mary said, "But he didn't escape, did he? Sir Henry put a bullet in his back just before my mother tossed me out the window into Uncle's arms, begging him to take care of me. He—he told me she backed away from the window then, not wanting anyone to be hurt trying to save her."

Rachel drew Mary into her motherly embrace. "That she did, child, and a few moments later the roof collapsed. She was a brave woman and she died with dignity, even if her husband's activities had caused her to live a life of horror."

"She *was* wonderful, wasn't she?" Mary said, smiling a little. "At least not all my blood is bad."

Pushing Mary away from her a bit in order to look her directly in the eyes, Rachel said firmly, "Now you listen to me, you foolish girl. Take all this business about 'bad blood' and wipe it from your mind. You are Mary Lawrence, beloved of Tristan Rule, and you have a glorious future in front of you. Don't waste time looking back—it serves no purpose."

"Tell that to Tristan, Rachel," Mary responded resignedly. "He must have cut his sleuthing teeth on stories of the evil Jules St. Laurent and the havoc he had wrought, the deaths he had caused. Even if Tris loves me, can he stand looking at me, knowing what he does about my father? Good Lord, Uncle Henry wouldn't even let me travel to France because of my father's reputation. Imagine the tumult if I went flitting about Paris, inquiring about my St. Laurent relatives?"

The bit firmly between her teeth now, she went on, speaking as soon as the thoughts hit her. "Not to mention, of course, the repercussions in the government if it were ever discovered that Sir Henry Ruffton, that trusted patriot, was harboring the daughter of one of His Majesty's greatest enemies. No wonder he changed my name and hid me away in Sussex!"

"I doubt that consequence ever occurred to him," Rachel replied firmly. "He told me all about you when he first asked my help in presenting you to the *ton*. Henry was always very open about things, you know. The love that shone from his eyes when he talked about you—why, he couldn't love you more if you were his own daughter."

"Instead of the daughter of his worst enemy," Mary interrupted, shaking her head in disbelief.

"Well, let me tell you—today we have buried
Marie Lisette Vivienne St. Laurent for all time. I
don't care for myself, you must understand. All
that talk about society doesn't mean a thing. I was
only grumbling about that to keep from thinking
about Tristan. But Sir Henry is too dear for me to
allow even a breath of scandal to sully his good
name."

"And Tristan, Mary?" Rachel asked. "How dear
is he to you? Will you allow him the gift of a little
time before condemning him for his reaction to
your news?"

A single tear found its way down Mary's cheek.
"I don't believe *my* forgiveness enters into it, Aunt
Rachel. I love Tristan, and he says he loves me. I
guess all that we can do now is to see just *how
much* he loves me."

The two women sat in silence for some minutes,
their arms wrapped comfortingly about each
other, until they could hear the dinner gong in the
hallway. "I'll meet you later downstairs, child,"
Rachel said, rising stiffly from the bed. "I want to
go down early to ease your poor guardian's
worried mind. He was feeling so guilty when I left
him."

Rachel's words caused Mary to remember Sir
Henry's good news of earlier that afternoon and
she grabbed the older woman yet again to give her
a warm kiss on the cheek. "My best wishes to you,
Aunt, on your upcoming nuptials," she congratulated sincerely. "I knew if only you two would sit
down and discuss things you would find your way
to happiness. What was the misunderstanding
anyway?"

Rachel smiled a secret smile. "We've decided to
let Sir Henry take all the blame," she quipped,
patting her hair. "He was feeling so downpin
about you that I thought it would take his mind off

at least some of his troubles if I gave him the forgiveness he was so eagerly seeking.''

"And Lord Hether-something-or-other? What about him, Aunt?'' Mary teased, remembering Rachel's slip of the tongue at the Venetian breakfast.

Rachel batted her eyelashes at Mary, the picture of innocent confusion. "Lord Who? my dear? I vow I *don't* know what you're talking about.'' She then clapped her hands together briskly. "Hurry now, Mary, or you'll be late to dinner, and Sir Henry has promised to bring out his best champagne in honor of our engagement.''

Mary refused to let her smile waver as she realized they could have been toasting a double engagement this evening if it weren't for Tristan's abrupt departure after hearing her news. "I'll dress now and then go hasten Kitty along,'' she promised, already ringing for her maid. "You know how long she takes when primping for her dearest Dexter. As if he'd even notice if she came into the room with a sack over her head, so besotted is the fellow.''

Rachel stopped just as she opened the door to leave. "Perkins said Dexter was here earlier today while I was out and you were closeted with Sir Henry. I'd worry about the proprieties, except I doubt either of them would know what to do in the first place. Dexter, for all his man-of-the-world claims, seems to be thoroughly baffled when it comes to dealing with innocents like Kitty. Ah yes, and yet another dandy succumbs to Cupid's leveling dart.''

Mary chuckled at the little joke until the door closed behind the departing Rachel. Then her features reassembled themselves into a solemn expression as she sent up a little prayer that Tristan wouldn't take too long to decide if his love for her was strong enough to outstrip his hatred for Jules St. Laurent.

Sir Henry and Rachel were just moving away from each other after enjoying a pleasurable embrace when Mary dashed into the drawing room waving a scrap of paper and laughing delightedly. "Kitty and Dexter have eloped to Gretna!" she exclaimed, tossing the paper into the air. "And I thought Kitty had nary a trace of spunk in her beautiful, dim head. Oh, this is wonderful!"

Rachel, now a betrothed woman, but still a chaperon, wasn't quite as delighted. Picking up the paper, she read Kitty's hastily scrawled note, that spoke of undying love and mean brothers. "And something about damp sheets, I think," she told Sir Henry, moving the paper closer to the light in order to better decipher Kitty's childish hand. "Who would have thought Dexter could engineer such a scheme?"

Sir Henry picked up his glass and took a small sip before saying softly: "Engineer it, yes. But carry it through to completion? Oh, no. Not if I know my man."

CHAPTER FIFTEEN

All plans for the evening were quite naturally canceled after Kitty's note was discovered, and Sir Henry sent a servant around to the Thorpe town house requesting the Rutherford's company as soon after the dinner hour as possible.

Although Dexter had reached his majority three years previously, it was common knowledge that Julian, who continued to provide his cousin with a generous allowance, was still unofficially in charge of the younger man. Added to that, Dexter was Julian's heir, at least for the moment, and Lord Thorpe would quite naturally be interested in Dexter's choice of mother to the next generation of Rutherfords.

Lucy and Julian arrived just as Sir Henry was rejoining the ladies after enjoying the solitary cigar he allowed himself each day. "What's wrong?" Lucy asked without preamble, dropping into a chair and settling the skirts of her ballgown around her—for she and Julian had been planning to attend Lady Cornwallis's annual ball that evening. "Your invitation was curiously lacking in detail. As I told Julian, it seemed more in the way of a summons. Pray tell me it isn't bad news. Have you heard from Jennie? Is little Christopher all right? Has there been an accident? I—"

"Hush, pet," Julian soothed, standing behind

her chair, a reassuring hand pressed to her shoulder. "How can we learn anything if you persist in cataloging the possibilities and giving no chance for anyone to answer yea or nay?"

Lucy looked up at her husband and pulled a face. "You were guessing too, sweetheart," she reminded him. "On the way over here in the carriage you had me half convinced Kit had taken a toss from his new hunter."

"I had a letter from Jennie just yesterday," Rachel put in before Julian could make his rebuttal, "and all the Wildes are as fine as ninepence. In fact, Christopher's just cut another tooth. It's just that something happened today—"

"Lucy, your Aunt Rachel has condescended to make me the happiest of men by consenting to become my wife," Sir Henry broke in, deciding he was not about to let Dexter's dramatic gesture overshadow Rachel's own news.

"Oh, Aunt Rachel, how perfectly marvelous!" Lucy exclaimed, jumping up and running to hug her relative. "May Jennie and I have charge of your wedding—and Mary too, of course? You can be married from Bourne Manor. It has the loveliest chapel, you know. Oh, we must start making lists this instant! When is the ceremony to take place? You won't want a long engagement, surely?"

Rachel took a peek at Mary, sitting slightly away from the rest of the group and looking so wistfully sad. "We'll wait until after Mary and Tristan's wedding, I think, as Sir Henry will be giving the bride away and we have already planned an extensive wedding trip through the Lake District."

Mary's cheeks turned chalk white, then rosy red, as she realized what Rachel had just made public. Rising to stand stock-still inside Lucy's enthusiastic embrace, she accepted everyone's best wishes in a small, wooden voice.

How could Aunt Rachel have done it? Already Lucy was asking why Tristan wasn't present, and Sir Henry, who seemed to lie with great ease, she realized, was accepting full blame for having sent the newly engaged man off on a mission that would keep him out of the city for at least a fortnight.

What if Tris decides to cry off? Mary screamed in silent panic. He'll never forgive me for making our betrothal common knowledge, not while the situation stands as it does now. He'll feel he's been trapped into going through with the marriage no matter what his feelings, if only to salvage his honor.

"I'm afraid our lovebirds here are rushing their fences, Lucy," Mary said at last, scrambling for a way out. "In their happiness they wish the whole world married. Tris has made an offer, it's true, but I haven't as yet formally accepted it. We're hoping this small separation will help us to be more sure of our feelings for each other."

"Fiddlesticks!" Lucy countered, crossing her arms against Mary's disclaimer. "You two were made for each other, and haven't Jennie and I told you so a dozen times?"

Julian, seeing that Mary was close to tears, cut in smoothly, "Put your arrow back in your quiver, Cupid, and promise Mary you won't breathe a word of Tristan's proposal until she wishes it made public. And that," he finished, tapping his wife gently on the tip of her nose, "also means you aren't to spill the soup in a letter to Jennie, swearing her to secrecy."

Putting out her full bottom lip in a becoming pout, Lucy reluctantly nodded her head before brightening once again as she begged to at least be allowed to be the one to give Jennie the joyous news once Tristan was returned and the engagement made official. "You surely don't mean to turn him down, do you, Mary?" she asked candidly, earning herself an admonishing "tsk-tsk" from her husband.

"You'll be the first to know my answer, Lucy, I promise," Mary sidestepped neatly. "Besides, although you believe yourselves to have heard all the news, you have yet to hear about Kitty and Dexter. They're the real reason we sent the invitation."

"Oh, yes, they aren't here, are they?" Lucy observed, looking about the large drawing room as if searching out the pair in a dimly lit corner. "That's strange. I had begun to think Dexter had moved in, seeing as how he's been camped on your doorstep day and night since Kitty took up residence. For such a dedicated flirt as Dex to have fixed his interest on a green girl like Kitty Toland fairly boggles the mind. Why, only last year he was amusing himself by pinching upstairs maids and chasing opera dancers."

"I'm afraid your cousin has done more than 'fix his interest' with Miss Toland," put in Sir Henry before Lucy could be off again, relating an incident concerning Dexter, her personal maid, Deirdre, and a large billiard table. "He and the lady in question are on their way to Gretna Green, to marry over the anvil."

"Of all the paper-skulled idiot stunts!" Thorpe exploded angrily. "How can he profess to be in love with the girl, and then proceed to ruin her reputation that way? There's a proper way and an improper way to go about things, and m'cousin has always displayed a marked tendency for taking the incorrect turning. But this—this is beyond belief. It's more than incorrect, it's—it's—"

Now it was Lucy's turn to calm Julian. "Low-

bred?" Lucy finished tongue-in-cheek before
Julian, displaying all the starch and arrogance
that had gained him the reputation of a high-nosed
snob, realized that everyone around him seemed
to be much amused, thoroughly enjoying his
momentary lapse into stuffiness—a legacy of his
privileged upbringing that marriage to the irre-
pressible Lucy had pretty much put to rout.

Julian smiled, as the ability to laugh at his own
foibles was yet another gift from his understanding wife. "Now that I've given you *my esteemed
mother's* opinion on Dexter's recent course of
action," he went on, once again positioning
himself behind Lucy's chair, "I believe *I* may have
a few questions. To begin—does anyone know the
reason behind this melodramatic flight?"

Mary produced the letter she had found but did
not bother trying to read all of it—most of it being
either unintelligible or embarrassingly unintelligent. "To sum up her note as best I can," she
informed Julian, "Kitty's brother Jerome, her
guardian, has refused consent for his sister's
marriage to Dexter. Rather than waiting out the
nearly five years until Kitty comes of age, Dexter
elected to spirit her away to Gretna, just like the
hero in some Theatre Royal comedy. I imagine
they've been on the road since early this afternoon."

Rachel spoke up then, apologizing to everyone
for her failure to adequately chaperon Kitty.
"How I could have scraped through without a
scratch with a termagant like Lucy, and then
failed so abysmally to ride herd on a wet-behind-
the-ears schoolgirl I'll never know," she mourned,
shaking her head in disbelief.

"You had other things on your mind today, my
dear," Sir Henry defended staunchly, lifting her
hand to his lips as Rachel blushed beet red,

looking much like a flustered schoolgirl herself.

Julian walked over to the collection of decanters residing on a side table and poured himself a drink. "Nobody's blaming anybody here," he said dismissingly. "If there's any blame to be placed, then I'd say we can safely lay it on Dexter's plate. What a devilish silly thing for him to do, no matter how pure his intentions. Has anyone thought to inform this Jerome person of his sister's flight? He may want to give chase, you know."

Mary spoke up then, telling Julian that an underfootman had been sent around to Toland's rooms but no one answered his knock. "We'll try again in the morning. I don't believe the two of them to be very close, however, even if Dexter was impressed with the way Mr. Toland used his gambling winnings to bring Kitty to town for a chance at a Season. I only met him myself by chance one day when he was here visiting his sister, but he impressed me as a man very much out for himself. He treats Kitty like a child, which she is of course, but he's not kind about it. She's always in the glooms following his visits." She shrugged. "I don't know. I have no siblings. Perhaps theirs is a commonplace enough relationship."

"You make him sound like a dog in a manger. After all, if he doesn't care for her, why would he turn down the chance to have her taken off his hands?" Lucy puzzled, turning to Julian for an answer.

"I'd be willing to wager a tidy sum that if Dex were more plump in the pocket, Toland would have handed his sister over to him on a silver platter—as long as he was handsomely rewarded for his trouble," he offered, earning for himself a snort of agreement from Sir Henry.

"Oh, that poor girl," Lucy murmured, her

tender heart touched by Kitty's plight. "I never realized before how very lucky I have been, being surrounded all my life by people who truly love me."

"And I," Mary added solemnly, looking straight at Sir Henry and Rachel as she spoke. "Having people willing to sacrifice their life for you, people prepared to protect you no matter what the possible cost to themselves, people caring enough to risk losing your love in order to help you see things in their true perspective rather than to only concentrate selfishly on how they affect you—I can think of no greater blessing."

Sir Henry swallowed down hard on the sudden lump in his throat. Finding Rachel's hand, he gave it a quick squeeze, whispering huskily, "I told you she was special. From the first moment I saw her, I knew. If Rules dares to hurt her, I'll have him stripped to the bone—I swear it."

"Tristan's your protégé too, my dear," Rachel reminded him softly. "He's had a shock, realizing he's tumbled into love with the daughter of nothing less than one of England's premier enemies of modern times. If St. Laurent had spied only for the French, serving his native country, it wouldn't be quite so bad. After all, what was Tristan himself, if not a spy? But a double-dealing secrets merchant who feigned loyalty to both countries while lining his pockets at the expense of the troops his misinformation as good as sent out to be slaughtered . . . well, putting that behind him is going to take a bit of doing."

Lucy and Julian, who had been discussing the possibility of intercepting the runaways and "negotiating" Toland's approval so that Dex and Kitty could be married from Hillcrest, Thorpe's country estate, hadn't paid much attention to the older couple's withdrawal from the general conversation.

As for Mary, she had once again descended into a brown study, believing everyone else in the world to be lucky in their love, while hers had been beset on all sides by unfortunate timing, sad coincidence, and outright bad luck ever since she and Tristan had first met.

Rachel and Sir Henry had seen their love triumph over time and misunderstandings. Lucy and Julian had faced down ugly rumor and a possible charge of murder to find a love that had enriched them both tenfold. Jennie and Kit had taken a forced alliance and turned it into a voluntary joy. Even Kitty and Dexter, as madcap and ill-advised as their elopement might be, had taken the first steps toward the happiness they were sure awaited them.

Only I, Mary mused ruefully, could have managed to be nearly seduced, proposed to, and then deserted, all in the space of a single afternoon. If Kitty and Dexter were playing out a Theatre Royal comedy, were she and Tristan resembling characters in a Haymarket melodrama?

Did they possess the patient love of Sir Henry and Rachel, the dogged determination of Lucy and Julian, the gift for giving displayed by Jennie and Kit, or the blind faith and trusting hearts of Kitty and Dexter?

Would Tristan be able to separate the Mary he had fallen in love with from the man he rightfully despised, or would he be defeated by his lifelong belief that people were either black or white, allowing for no softening shadings of gray? Could he put a rein on his quick temper and tendency to judge long enough to see that Jules St. Laurent, whether dead or alive, had only the power to hurt that Tristan chose to allow him?

Would she be able to forgive Tristan for his condemning attitude when faced with her true identity; his instinctive withdrawal from a woman he had just professed to love, but whose capacity for loyalty he might now always question? Could she cast off the shame she felt at having to own to such a father and leave her past behind her where it belonged, or would it always be there, lurking just below the surface, ready to raise its ugly head whenever she and Tristan quarreled, which she knew they would?

A sudden commotion in the hallway brought all five of the occupants of the room back to attention as Perkins entered to say that there was a "person" without demanding two pounds six for the rental of his hack or he would fetch the constable.

"A hack?" Sir Henry repeated, rising to his feet so that he could better reach in his trouser pocket for his purse. "Who in thunder engaged a hack?"

"I did, as a matter of fact," came a voice from the hallway, before Dexter Rutherford poked his head around the corner wearing his most winning smile and waggling his fingers in greeting. "Julian, do the pretty, will you? This oaf says he'll confiscate Kitty's satchel else. Hurry, do—there's no need setting the fellow's back up any more than it is."

"*Dexter!*" all five voices sang out at once, three in relief and two (the baritone members of the company) in exasperation.

"*Kitty!*" the three women then chorused as a woebegone little creature crept timidly into the room, her wide blue eyes red-rimmed with fatigue.

"Come here and sit down, dear," Lucy urged kindly, taking the younger girl's hand in hers and tugging gently. "You look burnt to the socket. What did that dreadful boy Dexter do to you? I swear he hasn't the wits of a flea. A hack, indeed! That cockle-head is foolish beyond permission."

"You found Kitty's note, I expect. It's either that or you're having a party and failed to invite me," Dexter remarked buoyantly, coming fully into the room once Julian had paid off the hack driver and secured Kitty's satchel. "Don't apologize. Kitty and I had ourselves a high old time of our own there for a while, bowling along lickety-split toward the north."

"And then you had second thoughts?" Mary prompted, thinking she was fast becoming an expert on such things.

Dexter laughed as he sat himself down at his ease on a small pillow he had dropped to the floor beside Kitty's chair. "I was never mad for the notion, you understand, but there was nothing else for it, so we were off. Second thoughts, you ask? It was nothing like. What sort of frippery fellow do you take me for—whisking a lady off to Gretna and then turning tail before we're halfway to the place? I have more bottom than that, let me warn you, even if there's many who'd try to tell you different."

"Whoever your detractors be, they may have my vote as well," Julian quipped nastily as he re-entered the drawing room. "Did you really think to ride all the way to Scotland, a three-day journey at best, in a broken-down hackney coach? Best plug up your ears, cousin, I do believe the stuffing's coming out of your brain."

"Oh, Gemini!" Kitty spoke up in her high, childish voice. "This is so prodigious unpleasant! You're all angry, aren't you? I told Dexter you would be."

"She's quick, I'll give her that," Lucy quipped, her cheerful grin taking the sting out of her words.

"It's all Jerry's fault, you know," Kitty persisted, willing to take on wild lions and tigers—or even a roomful of frowning people—to protect her dearest Dexter. "He was just being perverse, refusing his consent to our marriage. He doesn't really care a fig about me one way or the other. So what else were we to do?" she ended, looking to Sir Henry beseechingly.

"You might have thought to come to me, coz," Julian put in helpfully. "From what I've heard, Toland could have been bought off very easily, and then there would have been no need for your dramatic run to the border."

Dexter pulled himself up to his full height, although it added little to his consequence as he was naturally rather short and slight. "You would have me *buy* his consent, Julian? That's so—so—"

"Low-bred?" Lucy suggested, winking at her husband, who had the sensitivity to wince. "Nonsense, Dex, it's done all the time, and in the *highest* circles. But why, if you haven't had a change of heart, have you returned with 'the deed' still undone?"

"It wasn't for lack of determination, if that's what you're thinking," Dexter vowed, earning himself a watery smile from Kitty. "We ran short of the ready, as a matter of fact. I forgot I had paid some ridiculous sum on account to my tailor yesterday. It's so seldom I do silly things like that —is it any wonder it slipped my mind?

"Noticed it fast enough when I went to lay down m'blunt for our dinner at some pokey wayside inn, I'll tell you," he added feelingly. "Took my last groat to pay the fare, and the ham was stringy! The world's inhabited by thieves, do you know that? But that's not important. What matters is that now we won't be able to elope until my next quarter's allowance. Unless you'd care to advance me a hundred pounds, coz, in which case we'll be on our way again at first light and cause you no more bother."

Rachel pressed a hand to her mouth to suppress her mirth, as Julian's incredulous expression after hearing Dexter's meandering explanation—and most especially his last words—bordered on the comical. Just as Thorpe opened his mouth to deliver, Rachel was sure, one of his famous setdowns, she spoke up, saying briskly, "We'll discuss all this again in the morning when our thoughts are less muddled. Poor Kitty here is all but asleep where she sits. Mary, help Kitty to her chamber. Dexter, go home, dear—and take a bath. You reek of the stable."

"That doubting Thomas hackney driver didn't believe I'd make good on the fare and had me tending his broken-in-the wind nags for him at our last two stops. Said he'd be hanged for a Chinaman if he wasn't paid one way or the other," Dex explained happily enough, noticing a stray piece of hay sticking out from under his lapel and disposing of it in a nearby candy dish. "I'll go if you say so, Miss Gladwin, but I'll be back first thing in the morning to see Kitty."

"You will be in my study at precisely nine of the clock tomorrow morning," Julian contradicted heavily, "to discuss your plan to set Miss Toland's and your betrothal moving along more orthodox, acceptable avenues. Is that sufficiently clear, cousin, or shall I repeat it for you?"

Dexter winced as if in pain, knowing full well he was in for a verbal drubbing on the morrow that would doubtless leave him reeling. Nobody could rip you up quite like Julian, and he did it without ever once raising his voice. If he weren't so frequently the recipient of his cousin's blistering lectures, Dex might actually be able to enjoy them, for they were delivered with all the skill of a bonafide master of the art of insult.

"Can't we just pretend you've already pointed

out the error of my ways and forgiven me after
listening to my heartfelt apologies and instead
concentrate our efforts on bribing Toland into
seeing things our way, since I have your word for
it that such seemingly shabby tactics are within
the bounds of propriety?" Dexter proposed
magnanimously, willing to grasp at any straw.

"*Dex*-ter," Lucy warned, realizing the limits of
her husband's patience had been stretched nearly
to the breaking point. Poking fun at the foibles of
high society at Julian's expense would not be
Dexter's best choice if he wished to take up a new
hobby. She motioned her head toward the
doorway, and Dexter was quick to take her hint.
"Good night, dear. We'll look for you in the
morning."

Dexter grinned. If Lucy were to stand his ally,
perhaps the interview wouldn't be too painful.
"You'll be there?" he asked, his voice hopeful.

"I will," Lucy answered at the same time Julian
declared, "She will *not*." Dexter escaped while the
two of them stared at each other, primed to do
battle.

"Well," Mary observed lightly, having hurried
back to the drawing room after delivering Kitty to
her maid, unwilling to miss any more of the
proceedings than she could help. "It would seem
Dexter has found himself a champion, Julian. You
can scarcely tear a strip off his hide with your
wife standing there hovering over him like a
broody hen with one chick."

Julian merely shook his head in the negative,
winking at Mary. "Then I shall simply accuse my
cousin of seeking petticoat protection. *He'll* then
ask Lucy to leave, just to prove me wrong, and
then I shall give that young fool a lesson or two
that will serve to remove the spring from his step
for a space. Eloping to Gretna with only a few

shillings in his pockets. My God, the mind boggles!"

Mary laughed appreciatively as Lucy, knowing her ace had just been firmly trumped, stuck out her tongue at her smug husband. "I shall retire gracefully from the field this time, Julian, leaving you your small victory."

"You have to do that once in a while," she then told Mary blithely as she gathered up her shawl and evening purse. "It boosts a man's self-esteem. I try to make it a rule to let him win at least once in our every ten encounters." She grasped Thorpe's arm in both her hands and smiled up at him coquettishly. "Isn't that right, darling?"

Julian tipped up Lucy's chin with his index finger and dropped a light kiss on her mouth. "By the time you and Jennie are through tutoring Mary, poor Tristan is going to wish there was a nice, quiet war left somewhere for him to fight. Come on now, brat, we may as well go home. I'm no longer in the mood for dancing."

"Yes, my dearest, anything you say," Lucy agreed meekly before throwing kisses to Mary and her aunt and allowing her husband to lead her away.

"It bears repeating: how I ever survived the rearing of that imp of the devil is beyond me," Rachel said, sighing. "Come, Mary. We'd best go check on our returned prodigal. Henry?"

"I'll be here, Rachel. Waiting." Ruffton's voice was full of promise as he reluctantly released her hand.

There are a total of three newly betrothed females in the Ruffton household this night, Mary told herself as she slowly mounted the stairs. Kitty will most probably be already asleep and dreaming, confident her Dexter is equal to any problems that stand between them and their eventual marriage. Rachel, for her part, will doubtless soon be creeping back down the stairs to snuggle in the drawing room with her beloved Henry until Perkins coughs discreetly and sends her off to her dreams of wedded bliss.

And what of the third affianced bride? Mary thought self-pityingly. Oh yes, she will be left all alone in her bedchamber with her unhappy thoughts, doubtless the only newly betrothed female in all of England who will be crying herself to sleep this night.

CHAPTER SIXTEEN

The glowing tip of his discarded cigarillo drew a brief red arc in midair before disappearing into one of the high, unkempt weedy patches in what Rule's head grounds keeper had dared to refer to as the "informal garden."

He had been away playing at master spy too long, he told himself yet again—while Rule's Roost, his late father's pride and joy, had been left to the care of others. Pushing his body away from the ivy-choked brick wall he had been leaning against, he stepped more fully into the small patch of pale moonlight that was the only illumination in the cloak of darkness that served as cover for either the garden's or Rule's shame.

He had been at the Roost for three days, putting off the visit to his largest estate until last. By the time he had finished inspecting his horse-breeding property in Sussex and his orchards near Linton, he had thought he'd been prepared for the conditions he might find in Surrey, but the estate was in poorer trim than he had envisioned even in his worst predictions.

Oh, the farms themselves were well enough, as were the mills and the forestry holdings that had been his father's pet projects. Even though his inheritance had been thrust on him when he was still quite young, Tristan had shown the good sense to keep all his father's personal choices in their same positions of authority on the estate—bright young men who spoke of the "science of agriculture"—and his steady income over the years had given him no indication of anything being amiss.

Not that he would have tossed away his responsibilities to Sir Henry and the government even if he'd known anything had been wrong, he told himself now, shrugging his shoulders as he recognized the truth.

But the houses! And the grounds! How could he have been so blind? He knew his father's household retainers were already getting past it before he left home—after all, they had all been contemporaries of his father, or even older. One by one Tristan's housekeepers and butlers and gardeners had withered silently away, leaving the Roost and his other two houses to the indifferent mercies of young, mostly untrained servants whose main functions seemed to be equally divided between keeping their bellies full and doing as little work as possible.

Yet the worst, the very worst of it was not the overgrown gardens or the dusty furniture or the stained marble flooring or even the soot blackened portraits. It was the fact that everywhere he turned, every place he looked, he immediately thought, Mary could set this place to rights in the wink of an eye, and enjoy every moment of it into the bargain.

While he sat in the small dining room, picking at his solitary supper, he imagined Mary sitting at the opposite end of the table, laughing and teasing him, badgering him into eating all his vegetables.

As he mounted the first step of the wide, curving staircase that hugged the wall as it rose gracefully to the upper rooms he could see Mary descending slowly, taking care to lift the hem of her gown, coming to join him as they waited for the arrival of their dinner guests.

When he rode out across his lands, his heart filled with the pride of ownership, it was with the thought of Mary riding at his side, listening to his dreams for the future—dreams that included the enrichment of his properties, in order to provide a legacy worthy of the children that would someday ride these same fertile fields.

And when he opened the heavy oaken door to the master bedchamber he was careful not to let his gaze stray to the wide bed, where night after night he envisioned Mary lying against the plumped-up pillows, her auburn hair unbound and tumbling over her bare shoulders, her smooth white arms outstretched, a welcoming smile on her face.

Tristan covered his face with his hands, his eyes tightly closed, trying to blot out the scenes that appeared so clearly, even in this dark, shadowed garden. "A week," he muttered, anguish in his voice, "seven bloody-by-damn days! And it doesn't get better. *It gets worse!*"

"I murder him, I murder him not," Mary recited dully, stripping the petals one by one from the inoffensive bloom she held in her hand. "I murder him, I murder him not. I mur—"

"Oh dear," Lucy interrupted blithely as she peered around the partially opened door of the bedchamber and caught Mary in the act. "Aunt Rachel told me you had progressed from the doldrums to the heights, but I did not realize you were making plans to *do away* with poor Tris."

Mary tossed the denuded flower away from her and turned to smile at her friend. "You may rest easy. I shall murder him *not*, at least according to *that* posy's prediction. Not that the thought doesn't have some mild appeal."

Rachel, with Mary's permission, had already informed Lucy of exactly what was causing the breach between the lovers, and Mary had come to look forward to Lucy's daily visits—even if Lucy did persist in being disgustingly optimistic. "Well," Lucy said now, seating herself cozily on a wide chair, her toes tucked up under the hem of her gown, "at least you're not still glooming in your chambers, believing yourself to be some sort of Pandora and responsible for every ill to hit this world since the flood. Who knows," she added brightly, "given another day or two, you might just find you can face the world again—with or without my Master Grump cousin Tristan."

And it *had* been a difficult week for Mary. As Lucy had said, she had taken to her chamber, hiding herself and her shame away from the rest of the world. But it had been the loss of Tristan—and quite possibly Tristan's love—that had plunged her neck-deep into the dismals. Concern for her charge had prompted Rachel to apply to Lucy for assistance, for if there were ever a better person for looking on the bright side of things, Rachel couldn't imagine who it would be.

Lucy had more than lived up to her aunt's hopes, bearding Mary in her den—her bedchamber actually, but Rachel was fast becoming enamored of her own creative talents—and making the girl see that, although her late father was not the sort one would wish to have immortalized in oils for the family portrait gallery, it did not necessarily follow that Mary should shoulder any blame for her father's sins.

From there it was but a short step to the real heart of the problem: Tristan's reaction to the news. But that too was dismissed with a careless wave of Lucy's small hand. "It's all a nine days' wonder," she had told Mary confidently. "Tris was always marvelous at 'causes,' championing the downtrodden and fighting evil wherever it existed —even if it was only in his own firebrand mind. In his youth, Tristan viewed your father much like Robin Hood saw the Sheriff of Nottingham. Imagine poor Robin's reaction if his fair Maid Marion had been discovered to be the sheriff's daughter! Still, I am sure Friar Tuck would still have had a wedding ceremony to perform once Robin realized that, just like in all the stories, true love *does* conquer all."

Lucy's words had served to break the dam of Mary's emotions, and the two women had held each other while Mary laughed, then cried, then reached deep down inside herself and began to think clearly for the first time since that fateful day when Tristan had proposed marriage.

She had rediscovered her own worth, and had found reasons to be confident that Tristan's love for her—combined with hers for him—was enough to take them across the highest hurdle and gain them the happiness that waited on the other side.

But for Mary—who had not once in her memory been complimented for possessing a history of displaying ladylike patience—a week was time and enough for Tristan to have come to his senses and ridden back to town to claim her hand in form. While Rachel shook her head and voiced her misgivings to Sir Henry, Lucy looked on in amusement as Mary's feelings for Tristan ran the gamut from apprehension, to loverlike concern, to breathless anticipation, to impotent frustration, to—as the second week of Rule's absence began— downright anger.

"Stubborn baboon," Mary was saying now with

a decidedly militant air as she gathered up the scattered flower petals and disposed of them. "Not only could I box his ears for haring off to who knows where to leave me here with the whole mess of explaining his absence in my dish, but he is taking his sweet time in realizing that he simply cannot live without me."

Lucy peered at her owlishly. "Could this be the same watering pot who clung to my skirts blubbering something about having lost Tristan's love forevermore? I have to point out, my dear, that when it comes to self-confidence, there is little difference between you and my redoubtable cousin." She shrugged her shoulders and pulled a face. "But what do I know—as I have never been the shy and retiring sort myself."

"Wretch," Mary retorted amicably. "First you do your utmost to convince me that Tristan and I have a glorious future awaiting us, and then you browbeat me for my impatience to begin it. I was a fool to ever doubt that Tris would see that the past has less than nothing to do with us, I admit it freely, but please do not try to hoax me by delivering me a lecture on how I should not be angry with the man for stretching my sanity to the snapping point while he dithers about in the country scratching up the nerve to return to London and meet his fate."

"Bachelors never walk eyes open into the bridle, Mary," Lucy pointed out, speaking from her own personal experience as she pretended to inspect her nails, "but eventually they do all break to the saddle." Then, unable to hold her woman-of-the-world pose, she collapsed into girlish giggles, trying to imagine her dear Julian with a set of reins dangling from his aristocratic neck.

"You may laugh, Lucy," Mary told her, the light of battle in her eyes, "but Tristan is still heaven knows where and I am still sitting here stewing, waiting for him to come to his senses. I don't mind telling you that for every moment I spend contemplating getting a little of my own back for the misery he is causing me, I spend two fretting myself sick that he will feel it his duty to spend the rest of his life doing penance alone atop some far off mountain for the dastardly sin of falling in love with the daughter of his most hated enemy."

"It is a maddening mull, isn't it?" Lucy commented sympathetically. "Perhaps it is time I sent Julian to Tristan. A little man-to-man talk might be beneficial. Where is Tristan, anyway? In Surrey?"

"He can be in Jericho for all I care." Mary sniffed, feeling her recently acquired firm resolve to put a cheerful face on things beginning to crumble a bit at the foundation.

"Really?" Lucy asked doubtfully.

"*No!*" Mary rallied, hopping to her feet to cross the room briskly in answer to the knock that had just come at the door. "I asked Aunt Rachel that I not be disturbed unless it was something about Tristan. Do you think he might have at last settled all his demons and is even now waiting for me downstairs? Do I look all right? Oh, Lucy, I *don't* want to murder him, really I don't!"

She flung open the door to see one of the under-footmen standing in the hallway, a folded letter in his outstretched hand. Grabbing it with more haste than grace, she fairly slammed the door on the poor fellow's nose before skipping back to the bed, ripping open the plain wax seal as she wiggled her bottom into a comfortable spot in the middle of the satin bedspread.

"It's from Tristan, I just know it is!" Lucy declared delightedly, scrambling onto the bed to peer over Mary's shoulder as her friend read the contents of what was sure to be a most intriguing communication. "His handwriting was always as atrocious as my spelling," she said by way of excusing her nosiness. "You may need me to interpret for you."

But before Lucy could catch so much as a glimpse of the letter, Mary had hastily crumpled it and pressed the paper against her breast. "What's the matter?" Lucy coaxed gently, seeing that Mary had suddenly turned very pale. "It *is* from Tristan, isn't it?" Her eyes narrowing dangerously, she continued, her voice deepening to keep pace with her darkening emotions: "If that lamebrained looby has gone and done something stupid like setting sail to India to think things out, I will personally travel to Surrey to pull off his nose and stuff it in his ear! Of all the mad starts that idealistic moron has perpetrated, this one beats them all hollow! Why, I—"

"You can't pull off his nose, Lucy, if he is already aboard ship," Mary pointed out quietly, turning to look her friend in the eye. "Besides, this letter isn't from Tristan at all. The servant must have just assumed it was."

Lucy let out a deep sigh of relief before realizing that, whether the communication was from Tristan or not, it certainly contained *something* that had greatly upset her friend. She made a grab for the paper, but Mary quickly held it up out of her way.

"Lucy," Mary said earnestly, "your Aunt Rachel has told me what a scapegrace you are. If you will swear yourself to the deepest secrecy—promise not to breathe a word of this, even to Julian—can I count on you to help me?"

Lucy lifted her chin, willing herself to look competent and worthy of Mary's confidence. "Need you ask?" she pronounced dramatically.

"But what about Tristan? If you need help, surely he is the one to whom you should apply. Besides, it would certainly serve to send him hying back here to London posthaste, if he believed his fair damsel to be in peril from some dragon."

Mary shook her head, dismissing the idea, much as it appealed to her. "Don't make me think about Tristan right now, Lucy, as it will only serve to make me even more angry than before, seeing that it is his fault that I am in this coil at all."

"How?" Clearly Lucy was confused. "Will you please stop holding that letter above your head like some sort of dark cloud and tell me what is going on? *What* is Tristan's fault?"

Mary lowered her arm and handed the letter to her friend. "Someone must have seen me that night in Green Park while I was playing the spy for Tristan's benefit. I'm to buy this person's silence about my scandalous behavior by stealing some papers from Sir Henry's desk. I don't believe it, Lucy, it's almost as if Tristan wished this catastrophe on me! *I'm being blackmailed!*"

Julian Rutherford had always had a rather high opinion of himself, and even if Lucy's advent into his life had brought with it the realization that he was merely human after all, he was not about to believe that he had become so insignificant as to appear to be transparent.

Yet that was how he must have looked to his wife later that same night as he entered their town-house bedchamber with romantic dalliance in mind. Walking up behind Lucy as she sat before her dressing table absently drawing her brush through her dark locks, he leaned down to nibble delicately on her left earlobe, a location he had long ago discovered to be one of his favorite nuzzling spots. Needless to say, her response of,

"Julian, please, I have no time for that now," was not exactly the soft purr of pleasure he had been expecting.

He retreated a moment, then attacked from another angle, running his fingertips in soft, lazy circles slowly up and down her bare back, which lay exposed above the low neckline of her dressing gown. Lucy twitched her shoulders as if to shoo him away and complained, "Stop that, it tickles!"

Julian straightened, looking into the mirror at his wife's reflection. Uh-oh, he thought, remembering that particular expression on her face all too well. Loosely encircling her slim neck with both his hands, he asked in his most offhanded way, "Whose demise are you planning, dearest? Dexter has promised to abide by my decision to approach Toland with an offer I believe the man will find hard to resist, so you can't be plotting my maggoty cousin's next attempt at elopement. That leaves Tristan and Miss Lawrence, I believe. To be truthful, pet, I'd rather you refrain from poking your pretty little nose into Rule's affairs. I fear he might just take exception to your well-meant interference and break *mine* by way of retaliation."

"Tristan wouldn't do any such thing," Lucy argued, leaning her cheek against Rutherford's hand. "He likes you too much. At least," she added almost as if she were talking to herself, "he won't if he understands that you didn't know anything anyway, and therefore *couldn't* have told him, which you wouldn't because you're a man of your word, and I would make you give me your word before I told you—which I won't—so the whole question is silly, isn't it?"

"Dear me," Julian drawled after a moment of stunned silence, applying just enough pressure to Lucy's shoulders to have her rising from her seat so that he could turn her to face him, "I do believe I shall have to ask you to explain that last muddled statement. The only thing I have found to be worse than one of your harum-scarum ideas, my love, is to find out about it after the fact." Lowering his eyebrows menacingly, he prodded, "Lucy . . . out with it . . . *now*. I'm your husband, and wives should have no secrets from their husbands, should they?"

Lucy dropped her chin onto her chest, admitting defeat. "All right, Julian, I'll tell you," she said, sighing. Her voice was muffled against the front of his dressing gown as she added, "But you aren't going to like it above half."

He pulled her comfortingly against his broad chest, suppressing a manly smirk of satisfaction that would have had her ripping a good-sized strip off his hide if he had been foolish enough to allow her to see it. This marriage business wasn't so bad, he had discovered in the past year, just as long as he made sure to remind his wife occasionally just who was in charge.

Perhaps it was this preoccupation with his own brilliance in bringing his adorable widget of a wife to heel that blinded the Earl of Thorpe to the fact that his wife, now snuggling kittenishly beside him in the middle of their wide, comfortable bed, was smiling in a way that would have warned him that she was telling him only what she wanted him to hear.

CHAPTER SEVENTEEN

Tristan was in his bedchamber packing his belongings with a fervor only marginally concerned with neatness. For the first time since he had ridden his curricle neck or nothing out of London behind his blacks nearly two weeks earlier, he lamented his decision to leave his valet behind, preferring to sacrifice his comfort for speed.

But now, now that his hard-won decision had at last been made, he could only wish for Bates to be with him, so that the necessary packing—and a more useless, time-consuming exercise he could not imagine—could be taken out of his hands.

Wedging his new black brocade waistcoat down inside a satchel to rest cheek by jowl with one of a pair of muddy riding boots, he cursed himself yet again for being a blind, stubborn fool. How could he have—even for one moment, yet alone the better part of a fortnight—ever thought Mary's parentage meant anything? What sort of blistering idiot was he to toss away his only chance at happiness because Jules St. Laurent, dead and buried these last ten years, just happened to be the father of the woman he loved?

He had reacted, that's what he had done. What he had not done, he reminded himself with yet another swift mental kick, was *think*! Damn him for the hotheaded fool everyone who loved him swore him to be. He had behaved like some lily-pure candidate for sainthood who had nary a mar or blemish on his own record.

Well, nearly two weeks of searching his own conscience had revealed to him that not all of his actions during the past war would hold up very well under scrutiny. He may not have played both ends against the middle, he may not have acted only on his own behalf, and damn the lives lost by his treachery, but the news he so carefully ferreted out and sent back to Sir Henry had more than once resulted in someone's death. Indeed, there were several men now below ground that Tristan had personally sent to meet their Maker. Yet he had never stopped to ask himself if Mary could learn to live with the blood that was on *his* hands.

Jules St. Laurent had been a villain of the first water, there was no doubt about it. That he had succeeded in siring such a splendid, loving creature as Mary went against all the rules of nature, not to mention Tristan's long-held notions of right and wrong, black and white, truth and falsehood. But Mary did exist, and Tristan knew he could not love her more if her father had been the exemplary Sir Henry Ruffton himself.

If only it wasn't already too late. If only Mary could find it in her heart to forgive him for the damned presumptuous ass he had been that fateful day when he had learned of her parentage. "Oh, God, what a dolt I was!" he exclaimed now as he remembered how she had strode away from him that day, her chin held high, as he had bid her a stiffly polite farewell. "Pluck to the backbone," he said out loud as he threw his closed satchel at the servant who had just entered the room unannounced, thinking that any woman who could withstand the shabby treatment he had served up to her that day and not crumble was a jewel he could hardly believe he was worthy to possess.

"Move it, man, I want to be on my way before the sun rises another inch in the sky or know the reason why," he said to the servant, who had caught the satchel in self-defense and was standing there holding the thing as if he was still wondering how he had come to have it in his hands.

"But—but, milord," the man squeaked timidly (for all of Rule's servants, recipients of a rare dressing-down once the master had finished inspecting Rule's Roost, were more than a little in awe of their employer), "George jist come in wit some post, an' seein' as 'ow ever one's fer yer, Oi—"

Tristan suppressed an impatient oath and held out his hand for the mail pouch. He'd give its contents a quick read as he gulped down some breakfast and then be on his way. Loping down the wide stairs two at a time, he quickly scanned the letters, five in all, and felt a small shiver of apprehension skitter down his spine.

They were all from London. "And none of them," he muttered darkly under his breath, "is an invitation to tea."

Once seated in the breakfast room, he tore them open one after the other and read the signatures. Julian. Lucy. Rachel. Sir Henry. Dexter. *Dexter?* Good Lord, that scatterwit was so averse to writing that Tristan had once seen him ask the dealer in some gaming hell to scribble his vowels for him and he would then add his initials at the bottom. Something very serious must be going on if Dexter felt it necessary to take up a pen.

He threw down all the letters, then picked up the first that came to hand, which proved to be a mistake. Lucy's florid handwriting, overpopulated with swirls and curlicues, was nearly impossible to decipher, and her sentences, hinting of dire happenings, seemed to run on forever without saying anything at all.

His Aunt Rachel's missive was no better, which set his inner alarm bells to ringing all the more, for Rachel could always be counted upon to keep a cool head in a crisis, and Sir Henry's note, probably because he had long since perfected the art of concealing information, did no more than comment on the crowds descending on London for the coming fetes and request Rule's own presence for the festivities.

His appetite for the plateful of ham and eggs sitting before him having fled as he examined the first three communications, Tristan gathered up Julian's note in his one hand and stuck Dexter's missive in his pocket before heading toward the front door at a near run. He'd read the letters during his first stop for fresh horses, he told himself as he vaulted onto the seat of the curricle and snatched up the reins from the waiting groom.

But right now his years spent developing a sixth sense that warned him of impending danger served only to heighten his fears as he knew, deep in his rapidly beating heart, that Mary needed him —now!

Dexter was pacing back and forth across the Rutherfords' drawing-room carpet as his cousin watched in amusement. "I tell you, Julian, I had to do it. Ever since Kitty told me about her brother's past schemes—using her so shabbily to get himself inside the best houses and rob the inhabitants blind—I've been hard-pressed to keep silent. For he *is* her only relative, after all, and Kitty might take exception if I were to do something that would have the curst fellow clapped up in irons or something. But when she broke down and told me what Toland had said about Miss Lawrence—"

"It's all right, Dexter," Julian said soothingly, very much liking this new show of maturity his cousin was evincing, even if he didn't quite believe Dex completely comprehended the real facts in the matter.

"All right? All right!" Dexter exploded, throwing his slim body dramatically into a nearby chair. "If that don't beat the Dutch! How can you say so? I introduce Kitty into Sir Henry's household and the next thing you know her rum-touch brother is loping off with the family silver! But even the shame of such a thing pales into insignificance when you think the rotter may be trying to run some rig on Miss Lawrence. Lord! Tris will have my guts for garters, and no mistake!" Dexter prophesied grimly, dropping his chin onto his chest.

"So you felt it incumbent upon yourself then to write to Tristan directly and apprise him of a—um —*situation* that might require his presence in London?"

"You may tick me off for it, coz, but I really had no choice but to write to him, considering how I thought I'd like to keep my head where it is— attached to my neck," Dexter confessed, not caring that it was obvious that self-preservation had accounted for a good bit of his concern for Mary. "Besides, the ladies at Sir Henry's have all been acting as queer as Dick's hatband for the last week, always sneaking away together to whisper in corners, so it's Carleton House to a Charley's shelter that *something* havey-cavey is going on."

"Miss Gladwin included?" Julian pressed, finding it hard to believe anything too untoward could be occurring with that down-to-earth female around to keep Mary and Lucy from doing anything too outlandish.

Dexter sniffed, dismissing Rachel as having anything to do with the subject. "Miss Gladwin and Sir Henry are full of April and May, coz, and I swear, it would take more than a roof falling on their heads for them to notice that anything was amiss. Not that Kitty knows anything to the point either—the poor, innocent angel. I've just taken two and two and made four of it, that's all."

Julian allowed a small smile to escape his lips. "And they say there is nothing new under the sun. My goodness, you see me standing before you, amazed," he drawled, lighting his cheroot with a spill from the candelabra. "As to your compulsion to write to Rule and tell *all*, my dear boy, I must applaud you for your decisive action, and would give a great deal to see Tristan's face when he reads what I am sure must be quite an eloquent letter, considering your infrequent communications to me whilst you were up at school. However, as I too have felt the need to inform Tristan of the goings-on concerning his Miss Lawrence, I have no fears that we won't be seeing the fellow's dear, scowling face anytime soon."

That got Dexter's full attention! He jumped to his feet to confront his cousin. "Julian, you plague a fellow out of his mind, do you know that! You've let me ramble on and on ever since I got here, confessing my dearest Kitty's deepest secrets when there was not the slightest need for me to betray her confidence, when all the time you already knew something queer was going on. Remind me to do something especially nice for Lucy next I see her," he said acidly, "for how she has the fortitude to put up with the likes of you I'll never understand."

Thorpe poured his cousin a drink and then

slipped a soothing arm around the younger man's shoulders. "Heavens, I do believe you are somewhat incensed, bantling," he remarked cordially enough. "But before you go calling me out, let me tell you that although I am aware of what you call a *situation*, your information linking your false friend to it comes as quite a surprise. I only knew of a blackmailer. You, dear cousin, have given me a name. I commend you."

"Throw roses at his feet some other time, Julian," Tristan Rule advised tersely as he stormed into the room, still clad in his travel dirt. "Right now I want the bastard's name, so I can call him by it before I tear him into little pieces."

Dexter seemed to fold in on himself as he shrank inside Julian's comforting half embrace. "You can tell him without finding it necessary to jog his memory as to just who introduced Toland to Miss Lawrence, can't you?" he whispered pleadingly before ducking out from beneath Julian's arm and doing his best to blend in with the furnishings.

"Tris!" Julian covered neatly, crossing to Rule and holding out his hand in welcome. "You made good time, considering the state of the mails. I imagine you didn't spare the horses. No matter, Tiny and Goliath will see to them, I'm sure. I vow I shall miss those two when it comes time to return them to Kit. Come sit down and I'll ring for some refreshments. I'm sorry Lucy isn't here to greet you, but she's been living in Mary's pocket this last week, you know."

All through this prolonged greeting Tristan had been mumbling and grumbling, darting piercing looks in Dexter's direction that had the young man shaking in his shoes. "Did you ever try to make head or tail of anything that fellow has ever written?" he asked Julian as he accepted a glass holding a good three fingers of whiskey. "I've yet to decipher a word of it, or of Lucy's message for that matter, and Rachel and Sir Henry make a good pair, considering that between the two of them they managed to say nothing at all. Thank God for your note, Julian, else I might have been out of my mind with worry by now."

Julian acknowledged this faint praise with a nod of his head. "I can't tell you much more than I already have, I'm afraid. Lucy thought she could keep the blackmail scheme a secret from me, but I saw right through her, of course. She's promised to keep a close eye on Mary for me until you could return, but the blackmailer has yet to write again setting up a time and place for the information to change hands."

Tristan, remembering Lucy from their youth, narrowed his eyes and asked: "Are you sure she's holding nothing back from you? It's not like Lucy to be quite so helpful. It would be more in character if she were to combine forces with Mary and have the two of them plotting to capture this blackmailer themselves just to prove that they could do it."

Julian tipped his head to one side and thought about it for a moment, then shook his head. "Not Lucy," he said firmly. "She's a wife now, and past such nonsense."

"Rutherford!" Rule called, stopping the young man with the stern tone of his voice as Dexter was about to slink out of the room. "Two questions, if you please. One—considering your cousin's last statement, have you ever seen a pig fly?"

"Are you questioning my assessment of my wife's character?" Thorpe began heatedly. "Let me tell you something, Rule—"

"And two," Tristan went on unheeding, "give me the blackmailer's name, since you seem to have discovered it. In return I promise to try not to break your foolish neck!"

* * *

"Tristan's back!"

Mary, who had been standing beside the window looking out onto the street at the ragged urchin who was running off after delivering a second missive from the blackmailer, whirled about quickly, allowing the drapery to fall back into place.

"When? How?" she questioned, suddenly breathless.

Lucy dropped into a chair, fanning herself furiously with the glove she had just removed from her right hand. "I was just coming into the square when I saw his curricle pulled up in front of the house. It was a near-run thing, as Julian's coachman didn't take kindly to my order to have him return me to you so I could collect the glove I left behind—especially considering the fact that I had two gloves already upon my hands—but I knew you'd want to be warned at once."

"Warned, Lucy?" Mary questioned, tilting her head as if to better understand. "You were the one who swore to me that once Tristan came to his senses, he would rush to me and all but fall on my neck begging forgiveness. Why do I suddenly require a warning?"

Lucy lowered her eyes, trying to figure out a way of saying what had to be said without unduly upsetting Mary. "I wrote to Tristan, Mary," she began, only to be cut off by Mary's exasperated exclamation of disbelief. "I had to!" she insisted, flinging out her hands helplessly. "After telling Julian, it seemed the only safe thing to do. Think about it for a moment, Mary," she pleaded. "If Tris ever found out that Julian knew about the blackmailer and hadn't told him, and if you and I, perish the very thought, are discovered trying to capture this horrid blackmailer of yours—well, Tristan just won't like it if he finds out we all knew and didn't bother telling him, that's all."

"He'd punch your Julian square in his aristocratic nose, wouldn't he?" Mary agreed ungraciously, for Lucy's disclosure to Julian was still a sore subject between the two of them. "You realize, of course, that if you hadn't told Julian about the blackmailer, we wouldn't be in this coil now. I can only marvel that a mind so devious as to have the man believing you have told him the entire truth could have been so lamentably unable to keep the *entire* matter a secret."

"I was hoping Julian would take it upon himself to write to Tristan," Mary said in a small voice. "Men—you can never count on them to do what you want them to do. I checked the mailbag every morning for the letter, but in the end I had to take it upon myself to write Tristan. After all, if you said it once this week, you said it a thousand times —you can't wait to see the look on Tristan's face when he realizes that you've captured a blackmailer." Lucy spread her hands as if she had just made everything quite clear. "Well, you can't very well gloat over him if he's buried deep in Surrey, can you?"

Shaking her head in amused disbelief, Mary asked, "Are you quite sure there is no blood relation between you and Dexter? Your minds seem to work in the same illogical, harebrained way, you know."

Lucy snuggled more deeply into her chair and pretended to pout. "We can sit here all afternoon arguing, but what's done is done, and now Tristan is in London, and will doubtless be here within the hour, once Julian has told him everything he knows. As Julian believes me to be a spy myself, reporting all your actions to him, I am sure he will be able to defuse my cousin at least a little bit before he comes storming in here to tear you apart for not contacting him as soon as you learned of the blackmailer's existence. It's a pity we'll have nothing more to show him than that single letter."

"But that isn't all," Mary teased, waving the second letter in front of Lucy's face. "You know how you promised to help me, Lucy? Well, here's your chance. By the time Tristan runs me to earth I shall have taken care of the blackmailer myself—and saved Tristan from the gallows for having done the man in. Then I shall be more than happy to allow him to beg my forgiveness for having caused me all this trouble in the first place."

"And he will have realized once and for all that it can be very dangerous to jump to conclusions," Lucy added, reading the letter that called for an assignation later that same day for the purpose of exchanging Sir Henry's papers for the black-mailer's silence.

"It is nice to have everything coming together so neatly, isn't it?" Mary mused, wondering if it would be good form to wear her new blue walking dress to meet a blackmailer.

CHAPTER EIGHTEEN

Considering that it was born of necessity and formulated in haste, Mary's plan was, in Lucy's words, "none too shabby." Within an hour of Lucy's arrival with the information that Tristan was back in town, the two ladies were climbing into Sir Henry's closed town carriage, off to meet the blackmailer in a house just off Bow Street.

But alas, their departure did not go unnoticed. For just as the carriage was about to round the corner Lord Rule, with Lord Thorpe up beside him, came by tooling his curricle in the opposite direction. There was no doubt that the ladies had been seen and identified, a fact that was quickly substantiated by Mary, who looked out the back flap of the carriage to see Tristan wheeling his horses in a sharp turn, obviously set on following wherever the ladies led.

"We left it too late!" Lucy groaned, sinking back against the squabs in an attitude of defeat.

"Nonsense," Mary countered, already unbuttoning the top of her dress. "They are only following us because they know of nothing better to do with themselves. Why, we could be heading for the park for all they know."

"In a closed carriage?"

Mary wrinkled her nose at this reasonable question and quickly pulled the cords that lowered the privacy shades on either side of the carriage. "Don't quibble, Lucy, I'm nervous enough as it is. Now quickly, change clothing with me."

"What? Have you run entirely mad?"

"If we change clothes before we alight from the carriage, Julian will recognize your outfit and think I am you. that way I can meet up with Ben at the Bazaar as we have planned and you can lead your husband and Tristan off in another direction." Mary's bodice was completely undone by this time, and she was wiggling inelegantly as she tried to slip her dress down past her hips.

Lucy had chosen to pull her gown off over her head, so that her protest was faintly muffled. "But I'm supposed to go with you! How do you know the servants will be enough?"

Stopping what she was doing for the moment, Mary delivered Lucy a leveling stare. *"Tiny* will not be enough? Come now, dear, even you know that with Tiny and Goliath and Ben, you were only coming along for the thrill of the thing. Now hurry, I believe we're almost there."

"These bonnets are a godsend," Lucy said breathlessly, still huffing and puffing a bit after the exertion of completely changing her outfit within the confines of the carriage. "I vow I've never before seen such a profusion of ostrich plumes. No one will be able to recognize either of us from any distance."

Mary nodded, tying the ribbons of her own bonnet under her chin and arranging the plumes in a concealing fashion around the left side of her face. "I thought much the same thing when I saw them on Bond Street the other day. Poor Aunt Rachel, she couldn't understand my sudden ecstasy for drooping bird feathers, telling me youth has no reason to hide behind such frippery stuff."

The carriage slowed to a stop, and within moments the door was opened and the steps were let down for the ladies to descend to the flagway directly in front of the bazaar. Mary poked her head out first and immediately espied Ben standing off to one side, a resigned look on his face. "Hurry, Lucy," Mary then instructed, chancing a quick peek down the street to see Tristan furiously berating the driver of a wagon-load of wooden casks who was blocking the way.

Immediately after entering the bazaar, Mary thought, So far, so good, as Lucy went off in one direction and she and Ben in another. It may have been bad form to have gone into public without the protection of a maid or footman, but Mary didn't wish to involve anyone else in her conspiracy. Besides, as she was meeting Ben at the not quite so *tonnish* bazaar anyway, rather than at Sir Henry's house, there didn't seem to be too much danger involved.

Now that Lucy was to be set loose alone, however, Mary did take the time to experience a slight qualm about her friend's safety, but the thought that Julian and Tristan would soon catch up with her alleviated some of her guilt. All that mattered now was to get to the house near Bow Street, confront her blackmailer, and have Tiny hoist the man on his shoulders and carry him off to the constable.

She'd show Tristan that she was loyal to England, by God, and that she didn't need a constant watchdog to take care of her either! If she and Tris were to ever have a chance at happiness, they would have to begin as equals.

"Ben?" she asked, after following the bandy-legged servant onto a side street and entering the hack he had waiting for them there. "How far is it to Bow Street? Are Tiny and Goliath already in position? You are armed, aren't you?"

Ben answered her last question by patting the bulge that showed through his clothing. "Be there a'fore the cat ken lick 'er ear," he assured her as they bumped along the road. "We'll be met."

"Devil a bit of it, where are they?" Rule asked, exasperated.

Julian looked around again, trying in vain to pick out either his wife or Mary among the throng of shoppers, clerks, and pickpockets that jammed the narrow aisles of the large building. "Wait a moment, I think I see Lucy over there," he said, pointing off to the left.

"No," Tristan disagreed, narrowing his eyes for a better look. "But it's good enough, for it's Mary you've found. I think I recognize that gown. God, Julian, but that's a deucedly ugly hat. Why do women persist on wearing such things?"

As Tris spoke they were moving steadily in the direction of the waving ostrich plumes, closing in on the object of their search. "Mary's gown or nay, that's my Lucy," Thorpe persisted. "I may have overshot myself a bit thinking my wife above hoodwinking me, but I'll not have anyone tell me I don't know Lucy's body better than any man alive."

Rule might have dared a lot of things, but he wasn't going to touch Julian's last statement with a barge pole! In the end, it was academic anyway, for just as they came within three feet of their destination, Lucy turned about to face them, fear and relief showing on her face.

"Oh, dear, I'm in the suds this time, aren't I?" she asked, wincing a bit as she saw the scowl that had begun to furrow Julian's brow. "I'll beg forgiveness later, really I will, and I am prodigiously sorry, for it does begin to seem that this was a harebrained idea, doesn't it, though if you had

made the smallest push, Julian, I would have confided in you, even if Mary were not already in full
flight with her scheme, but for now I must tell you
that I am quite concerned about Mary. I—I think
she might require some assistance."

Julian shot a quick look at Tristan, who was
becoming alarmingly red of face, and grabbed his
wife by the arm to lead her back out onto the flagway. "You've had a second communication from
Jerome, haven't you? You promised to tell me if
there were any further developments. I'm exceed-
ingly put out with you, Lucille."

"Oh, Julian, don't go all stuffy on me." Lucy
pouted, thrusting out her chin. "Just say you're
mad as fire with me and have done with it. I—
what did you say? *Jerome?* You *know* who the
blackmailer is? Jerome *who?*"

"Jerome Toland, Kitty's brother," Tristan
ground out, whirling his cousin around to face
him. "The man's desperate for money. This isn't a
game any longer, Lucy. Mary could be in grave
danger." Lucy's determined chin began to
crumple as a prelude to tears and he relented a bit,
urging softly, "An address, pet, just give us some
direction."

Wiping roughly at her tear-wet cheeks, Lucy,
who would not have been so squeamish if it were
she herself who were in danger, but whose tender
heart was now filled with dread for her friend's
safety, said in a rush, "Jennie's three servants are
with her, Tris. You know even Mary and I would
not think to capture the blackmailer on our own.
It seemed so simple, you know. We would just
hang back and wait for the man to show himself,
and then Tiny would crack his skull or some such
thing and the deed would be done. It was to be a
bit of a lark, you see, and then you would have to
apologize for causing the whole mess by being

such a gloom-and-doom merchant in the first place. We—"

"An address, Lucille, or I'll turn you over my knee myself!" Rule threatened, having run out of patience.

"Julian!" she cried, appealing to her husband. "How can you let him talk to me like that?"

The Earl of Thorpe looked at his distraught friend, smiled slightly, and said, "I am afraid I must disappoint you, Tris. It is *I* who shall have that pleasure." Turning back to Lucy, he ordered sternly: "An address, madam, if you please. *Now!*"

Nothing was going as she had planned. In the first place, Lucy was not with her, which cut down on her enjoyment by nearly half. Having caught a glimpse of Tristan as his curricle had shot by, and seeing his dear, intense face again just before entering the bazaar, had succeeded in destroying the remainder of her spirits, although she took great pains not to look downpin around Ben, who she could see was ready to grasp at any straw in order to cancel the scheme entirely.

The house the blackmailer had designated for their meeting was a depressing sight as well, and a far cry from anything Mary had imagined when she had dreamed of capturing the fellow. For one thing, it was situated on a particularly nasty-looking narrow street, crowded with other tumbledown houses and more than a few low gin shops whose drunken, slovenly patrons spilled out into the gutters to either sprawl there unconscious or become sick in the puddles.

Mary had thought she could remain outside and let Tiny and the others take care of the actual apprehension of the blackmailer, but she could now see that there was no way to avoid entering the house herself if the man were ever to show himself.

She and Ben had just completed a battle of wills,
all fought in whispers, that had resulted in Mary's
decision to cross the street and enter the house
alone while the three servants found their way
into the building through the back door or a con-
venient window. Once inside—and after, she was
sure, being observed entering by the blackmailer
—she would stand there until she counted to
twenty and then return to the street, out of harm's
way until Ben signaled her that everything was all
right. The deed would be done, according to Ben
"afore yer ken say Jack Robinson."

Mary, her back stiff and straight, her ridiculous
ostrich plumes bobbing in the slight breeze,
walked swiftly across the street to enter number
sixteen without knocking, stopped just inside the
door, closed her eyes tightly, and began counting
aloud in a brave, if rather shaky voice: "One, one
thousand, two, one thousand, three—"

The hand that snaked around her waist from
behind squeezed tightly, robbing her of air, while
the second hand clamped down tight over her
mouth before she could give voice to the scream
that had already formed in her mind.

Obviously, she thought wildly as she felt herself being lifted off her feet and half dragged
up the stairs, the blackmailer has plans of his
own. Her eyes popped wide open in curiosity,
partly to see her surroundings, awful as they
might be, and partly in the vain hope that she
could see her attacker, who still held her
from behind.

Thankfully for her battered heels that had
banged sharply against every riser as they
mounted the stairs, the man did not climb to the
very top of the tall, narrow house, but stopped at
the first floor, kicking open a door and roughly
pushing Mary inside the room ahead of him.
Catching herself against the side of a rickety table,

she took a moment to catch her breath, and then turned.

"*You!*" she exclaimed unbelievingly as Jerome Toland closed and locked the door behind them.

Toland busied himself adjusting his lace shirt cuffs, which had been disarranged by his recent activities, and then made his captive a mocking bow. "One must make a living, Miss Lawrence," he said, shrugging. "Especially if one's idiot sister persists in falling in love with penniless men. You must understand I didn't set out to use you, but you played so easily into my hands that I found I couldn't resist. I apologize for causing you any trouble, and I'm sorry if you have suffered any upset."

"Oh, aren't you just!" Mary sniffed, remembering that she had never been very much enamored of this man, whose own sister did not seem overfond of him. "May I say, sir, that your concern leaves me totally unmoved."

Toland indicated the single chair in the room and suggested Mary sit down, but she shook her head and stood her ground. "I forgive you for those harsh words, Miss Lawrence, as I know this must be very unpleasant for you, but I believe we can conclude our business in short order. Have you brought the papers?"

The papers? Mary had to think for a moment before she remembered that she was to have brought some of Sir Henry's papers with her. Stupid! she berated herself silently. So sure had she been of the success of her plan that she had not even considered bringing along a false set of papers. She had nothing with her save her small reticule.

Tilting up her chin, she improvised quickly: "What sort of clothhead do you take me for, Mr. Toland? Of course I did not bring any papers.

After all, what assurance do I have that once the papers are in your possession, you will make good your promise not to make public my—er—indiscreet behavior on a certain occasion?"

"You stupid chit!" Toland exclaimed, slamming a fist down on the table, shaking the oil lamp he had placed there, and making Mary back up three paces and sit in the chair she had shunned earlier. "What the devil do I care what you do or who you do it with? You could ride stark naked down Bond Street for all I'd care! I need those papers! I already promised them to—"

Toland cut off his tirade as he saw Mary looking hopefully toward the closed door as if she believed it would come tumbling in on them at any moment. "You didn't come here alone, did you?" he asked in a low, hard voice. Crossing over to where Mary sat huddled in the chair, he grabbed her arm and gave it a mighty shake. "Who did you bring with you? Rule's not in London. I checked. Who is it?"

He shook her again, and she thought she could hear her teeth rattle in her head. "No—nobody! I *swear* it!" she cried, beginning to feel real fear creeping down her spine. Where were Tiny and Goliath? And Ben, where was he? He had promised her! She could have counted to a thousand by now! "Your note said to come alone."

Just as if the fates had set out to make a liar of her, there came the sound of running feet approaching outside in the hallway. "*Bitch!*" Toland cursed, and still holding tight to her arm, he swept a backhanded slap across her face, knocking her to the floor just as the door crashed open and Tristan burst into the room.

One look at Tristan Rule's face was enough to have Jerome Toland raising his hands in surrender, but Rule wasn't about to settle for turning the man over to the authorities. Toland had dared to touch Mary! He had hit her, *hurt* her.

Only one thing stood out clearly in Tristan's mind: Jerome Toland had to die. Tristan's hands bunched tightly into fists that ached to turn Jerome's handsome face into mush. "Defend yourself, you bastard!" he fairly growled.

Mary didn't know how Tristan had found her, and at the moment she didn't much care. All she could do was remain sprawled on the floor, staring in amazement as his beloved face turned into a dark mask of hate. So this is the man they call Ruthless Rule, she thought, at last understanding that Tristan's reputation was no trifling thing. When enraged, Tristan Rule would give pause to the devil himself.

Toland backed toward the wall, his head shaking slowly back and forth in the negative, until he was stopped by the edge of the table as it came up against the back of his legs. Reaching behind himself wildly for any weapon he could find, he grabbed up the oil lamp and sent it winging straight at Rule.

"Tristan, *look out!*" Mary screamed helplessly, scrambling to her feet as Rule ducked, and the lamp crashed against the wall. Immediately the straw pallet that lay against the wall was turned into a blazing pyre.

The old house was nothing more than tinder, and the fire, once begun, fed on it greedily. In mere moments one side of the room was transformed into a raging inferno. Tristan knew it wouldn't be long before the fire reached the doorway, effectively cutting off their only means of escape.

Toland must have realized it as well, for he made a mad dash for the safety of the hallway, slamming the door shut behind him as he went. Tristan only spared a moment to hope that Julian and Kit's three servants, whom he had brow-beaten into staying outside, would not let the man escape before turning his full attention on Mary.

If Mary had been shaken at the sight of Rule in a rage, it was nothing to the fear that raced through *his* veins as he looked at her now. For Mary was backed against the far wall, cowering in abject panic, staring unblinkingly at the rapidly spreading flames. She was more than frightened. She was terrified, frozen with horror.

"Mary!" Tristan shouted above the roar of the fire. "Come to me, sweetings! We have to get out of here!" As Tristan spoke, he tried to open the door, which had jammed shut.

She didn't move, except to slip down closer to the floor. Whimpering, she covered her head with her arms.

Again and again Tristan pulled on the door, but it was no use. "Damn it!" he cursed, giving the door a kick before turning back to Mary. Smoke was rapidly filling the room and he had trouble finding her in the dim light. Pulling off his jacket, he held it about his head and upper body as a shield as he made his way to her, then draped it around her hunched body. "Mary," he crooned, sensing now the full depth of her terror even if he couldn't fully comprehend the real reason for it, "you'll be all right. I promise. Let me help you."

But Mary had retreated from the room—from the fire. Feeling Tristan's arms wrapping around her, she began to rock rapidly back and forth on her heels, like an animal in pain—or a child in its mother's protective embrace.

Tristan lifted her unresistingly into his arms and stood up, moving toward the single window in the room. Kicking out with his booted foot, he splintered the last of the panes that remained in the already-broken window and looked down into the street. He closed his eyes a moment in silent relief as he saw Julian and Tiny standing below him looking up at the window. Jerome Toland lay on the ground beside them, Goliath perched on his back, as Ben stood over the captive, a nasty-looking club in his hands.

Putting Mary down for just a moment, he wrapped his jacket around his arm and hit out the spindly strips of wood that clung to the window frame. The heat coming from behind him was nearly unbearable, and the smoke rushing toward the open window caused him to choke and cough, as stinging tears threatened to blind him.

Mary was once again cowering on the floor, holding on to his leg like a terrified child. He had to use considerable force to pry her loose from her tight hold on him in order to haul her to her feet. Putting a hand under her chin, he raised her face to his, trying to make out her features through the smoke that swirled all around them. "Mary? *Mary!* Listen to me! I've got to lower you down outside the building, and then drop you. Tiny is waiting down there—Julian too. They'll catch you, darling, I swear they will."

She looked at him then, her eyes wide and unblinking, even in the dense smoke. "*Maman?*" she breathed, tentatively reaching out a hand to touch Tristan's cheek. She shook her head in the negative. No. This was not her mother. Who was this strange man? Where was her mother? She wanted her mother!

Mary felt herself being lifted, her body being moved toward the open window. The man was going to drop her out the window. *No!* She didn't want to fall; she *knew* the feeling of falling, that awful sense of hurtling helplessly through space. She wrapped her arms tightly around the man's shoulders, holding on to him for dear life, refusing to let go. "*Non, maman! Non!*" she pleaded over and over again as she burrowed her face against the man's neck.

Tristan felt his blood run cold. He didn't know what was happening, what had turned Mary into the little girl now clinging to his neck sobbing for her mother. All he knew was that they were both going to die in this burning hell of a room unless he could break through to Mary somehow, make her understand that they had to get out of here—now.

Instinct guided him, instinct and love. "Marie," he crooned softly, into her ear. "*Mon pauvre enfant, je t'aime. Allons!*"

"*Maman?*" Mary asked, tilting her head to one side, her arms relaxing a bit, allowing Rule to breathe more freely. She looked into Tristan's face for a long moment, clearly fighting to understand, and then suddenly, her face crumpled in sorrow. "*Maman* is dead. Oh, Tris, my mother is dead!" she cried, as her memory, and complete realization of what had happened finally hit her. And then she fainted.

Tristan clasped Mary to him tightly, thanking every deity he could think of for the joy of hearing his name once more on her lips. Tears streamed down his soot-darkened face as he rained small kisses against Mary's cheeks and neck, until the loud crash of a ceiling beam breaking away and hitting the floor behind him brought him back to his senses.

He gave Mary one last kiss, then holding her limp, unconscious body by the wrists, he lowered her out the window as far as possible before dropping her to the street below, where Tiny stood waiting. The gentle giant caught her neatly as she fell and quickly handed her over to Julian before turning his attention once more to the first floor window.

"I be waitin', milord," he shouted in his big voice. "*Jump!*"

JULY 1815

"Christopher Wilde, you come back here at once!"
Jennie's only acknowledgment from her offspring
came in the form of a childish giggle, before the
boy was off again, running as fast as his chubby
legs could carry him, his nursemaids, Tizzie and
Lizzie, huffing and puffing along behind in hot
pursuit.

"Let him go, dearest," Kit said lazily, not
moving from his lounging position up against the
base of a comfortable shade tree.

"Only a man would say such a thing," Jennie
retorted. "He'll get grass stains all over his new
outfit—and he looked so adorable in church too."
Turning to her cousin Lucy, now carrying her first
child and more likely to be sympathetic to Jennie's
motherly pride, she said, "He made the perfect
ring bearer, didn't he?"

Julian Rutherford, who had been busying
himself arranging a pillow at his wife's back as
she sat in a soft, upholstered chair he had ordered
carried out onto the lawn for just such a purpose,
replied tongue-in-cheek, "He certainly did, Jennie.
I especially liked it when he refused to turn over
the ring to the vicar."

Kit chuckled deep in his throat as he lay with his
hat tipped front over his eyes, earning himself a
playful jab in the ribs from his wife's slippered

foot. "Hey!" he protested, raising the brim of his hat an inch to smile up at Jennie.

Lucy patted her protruding abdomen and said soothingly, "Don't worry, sweetings, your aunt and uncle are only funning." Pretending to be stern, she warned her cousin and her husband that they were setting their as yet unborn relative a bad example.

"They don't have to, Lucy, with you as the poor child's mother," Rachel quipped lightly, just then walking up to the group arm in arm with her brand-new husband. "Why do you think I married Henry in such a rush after Waterloo? The mere thought of having to bear-lead your sure-to-be harum-scarum offspring had me begging the poor man to give me the protection of his name."

Sir Henry Ruffton, his cherubic face beaming with pride as he gazed at his bride, refused to be insulted and merely pulled her more fully into his embrace and kissed her on the cheek. "We could have been wed months ago if it weren't for that devil Bonaparte breaking loose from Elba just after Mary and Tristan returned from their wedding trip."

The group was silent for a few moments, each reliving the horror of those awful "hundred days," when Bonaparte roamed Europe again and it seemed that another long, hurtful war had begun. The three women exchanged looks, each remembering the long months when their men, along with Tristan, were gone from their sides, off defending their country.

But Bonaparte was well and truly defeated this time, and plans were already in train to have him banished to St. Helena, where many had said he should have been imprisoned in the first place. The men had all been home for nearly a month and

Rachel and Sir Henry had at last been married from Rule's Roost, with Mary and Tristan acting as hosts to the bride and groom.

"Where are Tris and Mary?" Lucy asked now as her thoughts led her to notice their hosts' absence. "Surely Kitty and Dex are long since gone on their way."

"Mary must have had something to do in the house after waving our other lovebirds good-bye," Jennie guessed, shaking her head as she remembered Dexter's barely suppressed eagerness to be on his way, anxious to have his bride of one week to himself once again.

Julian leaned down to whisper to Kit under his breath. "Bet they don't make it any further than the nearest inn."

"As long as it doesn't have damp sheets," Kit quipped, and the two men laughed at the shared joke as their wives shook their heads at such nonsense.

Upstairs in Rule's Roost, far from the festivities taking place on the sunlit lawns below, Mary and Tristan Rule stood locked together in a quiet embrace, relishing the momentary respite from their duties to their houseguests.

"Aunt Rachel looked beautiful, didn't she?" Mary murmured into Tristan's shoulder, rubbing her cheek against the fine satin of his jacket. "So many delays, so many years wasted. Thank goodness she and Uncle Henry are together at last."

Tristan's arms tightened fractionally around Mary's slim body as he thought about the time he had wasted fighting his love for her, and how his realization of that love had nearly come too late for both of them. "She insisted on waiting until you had recovered your strength and she could organize our wedding," he recalled, placing a kiss on Mary's hair. "I never truly appreciated my aunt's worth until I witnessed her care of you after the fire. She was magnificent."

Mary closed her eyes, remembering the long weeks it had taken her to come to grips with the memories the fire in the house off Bow Street had released in her mind. "She didn't do it alone, you know," she teased, looking up at her husband with love shining bright in her green eyes. "I seem to recall a rather handsome gentleman who came to call daily, bringing me flowers and pretty trinkets."

Tristan smiled down on her, his harsh features softening. "And do you remember a certain small cottage near Linton where that same 'handsome' gentleman spent six wonderful weeks trying to show you how very much he loved you, how very much he will always love you?"

Pulling her brows together as if trying very hard to recall such an incident, Mary asked, "Would that be the same man who then deserted me this past March to spend the entire spring transporting messages back and forth across the channel from Brussels? I do believe I remember him faintly."

"I've been home for over a fortnight!" Tristan objected in mock anger, sweeping her up into his arms to hold her high against his chest. "You know we've scarce had a chance to breathe, let alone be alone above a few minutes at a time. Can I help it if the place has been thick with relatives and servants scurrying everywhere preparing for the wedding?"

Mary tilted her chin down and looked up at her husband through her lowered lashes. "We're alone now, Tristan," she purred invitingly, enjoying the color that her words brought running into his lean cheeks.

"But our guests —" he began, his eyes darkening

as he remembered the collection of relatives waiting for them.

"What about our guests?" Mary taunted, reaching up to nibble on a corner of his lips with her small, white teeth. "Be ruthless, Tris. Let them fend for themselves for a while."

Tristan spared only a moment to look out the window at the people relaxing beneath the shade tree before turning on his heels and carrying Mary over to the wide bed that lay waiting in the master chamber.

"My Lord Tristan Rule vows *he* is no fool!" he quoted softly as he lowered his wife onto the counterpane and the people waiting on the lawn, the memories of the past, and, indeed, all the rest of the world faded joyfully away.

About the Author

Michelle Kasey is the pseudonym of Kasey Michaels, which is the pseudonym of Kathie Seidick, a suburban Pennsylvania native who is also a full-time wife and the mother of four children. Her love of romance, humor, and history combine to make Regency novels her natural medium. *The Ruthless Lord Rule* completes her trilogy—including *The Beleagured Lord Bourne* and *The Toplofty Lord Thorpe*—for Signet Books.